ALASKAN DAWN

RICHARD EVANS

Alaskan Dawn
by *Richard Evans*

Signalman Publishing
www.signalmanpublishing.com
email: info@signalmanpublishing.com
Kissimmee, Florida

ISBN: 978-1-935991-79-3 (paperback)
        978-1-935991-80-9 (ebook)

R3

Printed in the United States of America

SIGNALMAN
PUBLISHING

PROLOGUE

In a reflection of attempting to comprehend why we exist.

We try so often to find the divine reason for our existence and wonder at least once in our lifetime why we were placed in our present state, time, and course in history. As finite human beings, we often come to the assumed conclusion that fate can be overcome by our own will and decisions. But is so often the case, our destiny depends on our parents, the time and place of our birth, and our God. As God uses his astute pronouncements, that destiny may be thrust upon us with an unexpected and sudden impact. Life is too short not to follow the path we were created to follow. To alter that path is to incur additional difficulties that we were not meant to have. Every man has the capability for greatness, but his strong impact upon this earth cannot always be judged immediately. It is born out of our inherent desire to seek awareness of what life offers us. We use our abilities to show the world what type of individual we shall be and always have been.

It is the will of the molder at those needed times, to shape us with fire to demonstrate if we are a workable composition of his loving handiwork. It is his desire that we are fashioned into a formidable human being that is able to withstand the multitude of inferno desires of this world. The pattern of our own lives was sketched in stone years before we were ever born. To ride on the winds of aspiration and prestige and triumph would never overshadow what was already formed and shaped in the furnace of the maker. It is from this possibility that this story has its basis.

CHAPTER 1

December 4, 1941
Aboard a train in South Central Siberia

Fourteen-year-old Alexander Baranoff's eyes shot ahead as the muffled sound of breaking glass shattered the steady harmony of the mesmerizing and perpetual clacking rhythm of the train wheels beneath his feet. In semi-cautious bewilderment, the slender brown-haired youth tried to position his body to where he could hear what action was going on inside the next car.

It was hard for the young teenager to hear much of anything for the simple explanation that he was standing outside between the jaunting railway cars in the icy tempest that was coming south across the tree-lined taiga of the vast Siberian plain. Combined with the noise of the locomotive, the cold wind was nearly deafening. Tightly interlaced passing Russian Birch and Latyshev pine trees of the taiga stretched on either side of the track. The branches and limbs of the evergreens were heavy laden with huge round balls of snow that made the trees look like a stacked bundle of huge cotton balls. The thick foliage made the night seem even darker as they darted in a long column on either side of the train. It was like a long dark tunnel without a roof.

The young man winced as the frosty snowstorm whipped an icy blast that felt like small pin pricks of several needles into his face. The wind was an indication that it was time to get out of the cold. The teenage boy once again placed his ear against the closed door to hear the disquieting noises that emulated from inside the railway car.

The young Russian lad yearned for the unusual distraction; the trip across Russia up to this point had been tedious and long. He had little understanding for the reasoning of his father's trip to America for lend-lease aid.

The disturbance Alexander heard next on the inside of the car was rather out of the ordinary. It was quite different from the train's usual movements of which he was a passenger. The disruptive sounds broke the steady monotony of the locomotive and the calmness of the moonlit night.

The young Russian teenager stopped in his tracks. What he overheard just on the other side of the door was horrifying. There was a shrill wailing screech, followed by a stifled and muffled groan. The blood curling sound could be heard beyond the door that he was about to enter. The young man tried to peer around the side of the jostling car into a side window. The bitter wind prevented him from looking too long. The dark green painted railroad cars from the side view looked almost black in the dimness of the night. The color of the dark engrained wood added to the chill and dread of Alexander's thoughts.

The young Russian boy stepped back to the outer door and stooped down to see through the window. The dark brown curtain on the other side of the glass was drawn all the way and he could not see what was happening inside.

"That sounded like someone is really in pain." he rationalized in his mind. "What could have happened? Could someone be hurt in there?" The thought made him hesitate, but curiosity overcame his easily yielding judgment. He stood transfixed, unable to make up his mind. Through the cold wind of the car platform of the Trans-Siberian train, the ruddy-cheeked fourteen–year-old boy turned his head. In twisting his head and bringing his ear in out of the wind, Alexander tried to distinguish between the wind and the pounding awful noises inside the passenger car.

Tilting his head briefly, Alexander pressed his ear against the door and listened again. All he could hear now was the steady rhythm movements of the wheels of the train on the track below him.

Caught between curiosity and concern, Alexander quickly weighed the possibilities and consequences in his mind. The medium built, but somewhat lean youth decided to investigate. His brown hair beneath the hood of his heavily padded coat poked its way out to his brow, blowing to and fro in response to the brisk wind.

Alexander's other option was to head back to his father's drawing room, but he quickly dismissed that notion. Besides it was far too cold to stand outside on the atrium between the two rail cars. The bitterly cold wind filled his lungs and it was slightly painful to breathe. The air also contained traces of black soot coming from the locomotive. The putrid stench of the windy mixture of frosty air and coal smoke was quite unpleasant. It was impractical to stand outside and freeze much longer.

Alexander blew warm air into his hands as the wind penetrated his gloves. His round face was bright pink with the frosty tinge of the night air. His skinny frame shivered. The cold wind was a great motivator for going in the dark and murky car.

"I need to see what is happening in there," he thought as he reached slowly for the white handle of the door. Perhaps it was his inexperience in predicting danger or maybe his seemly unending boredom that dulled his instinct to stay out of harm's way. In any case, his sense of intrigue overshadowed his common sense. "I have to see what has happened," he repeated again in his mind. "Maybe I can help?"

His teenage judgment prevailed and the decision was made. He opened the door slowly.

Alexander Baranoff stumbled as he entered the fourth passenger compartment of the train. The swaying motion of the train made him lose his balance and he fell into one of the double bed staterooms, partitioned off only by a red blanket hung up to serve as a door. The air was stale with the smell of the old blanket that obviously had not been washed for a long time. Alexander frantically grabbed for the red blanket in an attempt to steady himself, but his grasp was in vain. Tumbling to the floor, Alexander put his hands out as he stumbled over a large unseen object. The room was nearly pitch black, but the young teenager knew immediately that he had fallen on top of a human being lying on the floor. Alexander was annoyed that the man on the floor didn't even have the proper manners to attempt to move out of the way.

"I'm sorry!" stammered the young Russian, groping his way through the darkness. "What are you doing here anyway?" Alexander's eyes had not yet adjusted to the dimness of the interior of the railway car.

Alexander quickly surmised that he was not at fault here. "You big oaf. My father will have your hide for this." The immediate impact of the situation made him feel that something was not quite as it should be.

As Alexander used his hands to lift himself off the still unknown man's body, a sudden realization penetrated his mind—the man was dead.

Alexander picked himself up and he switched on a nearby incandescent light. He gazed momentarily at the Russian soldier's body, and then by instinct his eyes went from side to side to see if anyone else was with him in the dead man's sleeping quarters. Alexander knew that someone had coldly murdered this man only a few minutes earlier.

Alexander's throat tightened. There had been not enough time for anyone to shuffle out of the compartment that fast.

Panic quickly set in the boy's eyes. He was afraid that the killer was still in the same compartment with him. Alexander glanced at the dead soldier's body to see what else had happened.

The blood was still fresh on the brown uniform, but there was a great amount of evidence to suggest that a huge struggle had taken place between the soldier and his assailant. Three vertical puncture marks were embedded in the man's back and chest. Red blood was flowing freely from the wounds and it had been splattered on the dark brown oak floor of the corridor. The rectangular brown cap with red trim was clear on the other side of the room from where the body had been found. Bed sheets had been crumpled and an overhead lantern had been smashed. A nearby broken mirror clearly showed that the guard had not died immediately. A yellow mangled curtain from a nearby window had been pulled down where it had stayed in the grasp of the dead soldier.

Alexander was used to bodies, but not in this section of Eastern Siberia. His hometown of Leningrad had been littered with death ever since the Nazis had begun their invasion of Russia five months earlier. The image of the war-torn zone of Leningrad was enough of a reminder of dead bodies. Alexander had hoped that he had escaped seeing any more mutilated bodies.

As he turned to find help, a thump at the far end of the railroad car distracted him.

The faint sound gave rise to perking the young man's ears into sobering awareness. Coming to his senses after the initial shock of finding the body, Alexander quickly turned off the light and threw himself to the hard floor.

Alexander shifted his eyes to the far end of the obscure dark railway car. He could only catch quick glances of the far end of the car with the passing lights outside of the train that swept by in intermittent waves.

It was then Alexander noticed a slight motion in the darkness. Alexander had turned off the light in quick response and his eyes had not had time to adjust to the darkness. Squinting, Alexander saw a murky figure of a shadow moving about at the far faded end of the car. Immediately a disturbing thought entered his head. "Maybe the killer is still with me in this car." Alexander swallowed hard trying not to show his nervousness. He could hear his own heart beating faster. Alexander was positive that the assassin at the far end of the rail car could sense and see his every move.

Not wanting to be the killer's next victim, Alexander closed a nearby window shade that was splashing moonlight upon his face. He started to crawl towards the door that he just entered.

The young Russian teenager was nearly to the door and reaching up for the handle when an additional faded light from a far room was suddenly extinguished. Alexander dropped lower to his knees instinctively. The railway car was completely dark now. The only noise that could be heard was the rhythmic clack-clack of the steel wheels below him.

As Alexander turned his head to pick up even the slightest noise, a sudden but faint thud echoed in his ears on the wall right above him. Alexander winced as he tried to avoid the encounter of the single thumping noise. It made the teenager duck even lower. Alexander tried to make out what had caused the noise, but it was too dark to see anything. The young Russian looked behind him to see if there was anything at the other end of the car, but all he could see in the darkness was what appeared to be another moving shadow.

"Who's there?" he called out, hoping to scare off the intruder. Raising his head slowly, Alexander caught a quick glance of a darkened body moving swiftly. The only response he received from his question was the slamming of a door from the far end of the rail car.

Frightened, Alexander hastily retreated out the nearest door, back towards the car where his father's guards were stationed.

Within seconds Alexander had reached the vanguard of the elite Russian army troops in the sectional car up near the locomotive, but it took another four minutes to convince them that a dead soldier was at the other end of the train.

Finally the young man persuaded them to go back and look. Alexander discreetly followed them back towards the dead man. It would take a couple of minutes because most of the Soviet soldiers had situated their living quarters three cars away down near the locomotive.

Soon the train was full of commotion where Alexander had run off to find help. Soldiers methodically looked for nearby rifles, still wondering if the death was real.

The situation however was quite different in the railway that contained the dead body where a Nazi killer in a Russian uniform quickly came out of hiding. At the other end of the train in the dimly lit car, the medium-sized individual slipped back into the grisly death site. He glanced quickly at his victim on the floor and stepped over the fallen Russian soldier. Spitting on the dead man, he bolted through the door that Alexander had just run through. The Nazi agent correctly assumed that it would be too easy for others on the train to identify him if he had stayed at the far end of the train. There were only five men in that part of the train. They all had the excuse of being together. If a man had joined them with bloody hands, they would have picked him out as the killer right away.

The frightened man slipped into the next sleeping car. Scanning the aisle towards the engine, the murderer quickly slid in and opened a nearby hanging curtain of a nearby bedchamber.

The man quickly entered the bedchamber and filled a washbasin with water. He was going to make sure that this hideous crime wasn't pinned on him. He quickly removed his bloody clothes and washed his hands. His bloody clothes were tossed out the window. He assumed correctly that wild animals along the tracks would drag them off. A fresh uniform hung on a hook. He put on the clothes and waited.

The murderer wanted to be with the soldiers when Alexander brought them back. He would slip in behind them from one of the adjoining staterooms as the soldiers went by. The plan was foolproof. The only suspects would be in the fifth and the last car.

It was only a few minutes later that Alexander had made it back to the car where the dead body was lying as the squad of soldiers began surveying the bloody scene.

"Go check the last car," an officer ordered.

One of the soldiers responded and headed to the last car, hoping to catch someone with bloods on his hands.

Alexander could not help but stare at the dead soldier's body as the Russian security guards started to investigate the immediate area near the slain man's body. The young Russian had seen how deep the three knife wounds had penetrated and wondered who could have been so unusually cruel and violent.

Alexander closed his eyes. His mind raced back to a few weeks earlier when he was preparing to leave Leningrad with his parents. In his mind, tortured thoughts prevailed and the young Russian remembered all too vividly the people who had died from starvation and from German artillery. There seemed to be dead bodies heaped everywhere. Some of those who had died had been close friends and relatives. "I thought I would never see death caused by war again, not like this!" Alexander bit his lower lip, trying to push out the horrible images of his closest friend, Nicholai dying out of his mind.

It was no use. Alexander could see the moment of the death of his best friend as clearly as if it had happened that very day. The vivid image of his friend coming to see him and dying as a shell hit nearby made his stomach cringe. Alexander remembered the very place he was standing as the explosion occurred. He had just stepped out the door of the family home and had turned to utter a greeting to his best friend coming to visit. The sudden explosion had killed his companion instantly. "Nicholai didn't even have a chance to respond," Alexander remembered. "Those German pigs. Now it appears that one of those animals is out here in eastern Russia." His hatred of the Germans had intensified since he had seen his friend killed. "Can't I ever get away from their brutality? I hate those dirty scoundrels." He rubbed his chin with the back of his hand. "All Germans are nothing but scum. I'll make them all pay." Thinking about what his friends and relatives were going through now back in Leningrad made Alexander briefly realize that he was quite lucky. Seeing his best friend obliterated by a German artillery shell just a few yards in front of him was frightening, but Alexander knew he was away from the bombing now. He shuddered. "How many had died?" he agonizingly asked himself.

"You were lucky, Alexander!" The young Russian was jolted from reminiscing. He raised his eyes over to where Lieutenant Zaronavich pointed to the place where Alexander had heard the dull thud in the darkness above his head. A slim dagger with a Nazi insignia was impaled in the wall near the door.

Alexander grabbed his neck, realizing the soft thud he had heard when he ducked earlier was a knife hitting the wall that had been thrown at him by the assassin.

Alexander gulped. He had just barely escaped death. His mind raced with the possibility of his demise

"What happened here?" bellowed a voice from the outside on the atrium leading from the forward compartment. The entire carload of people glanced simultaneously to the front of the rail car. There was an unsettling and brief silence that encompassed the immediate area. It lasted only a few seconds.

Out of respect and some fear, there was no one who dared answer the question. The only sound in response was the steady clack-clack of the train. Eyes shifted uneasily from soldier to soldier. The man's impatience erupted and temporarily broke the steadiness of the rhythm. "Well," demanded the large man with the barrel chest and piercing dark eyes. His moustache bristled. "I want an answer!"

Alexander recognized the overbearing voice could only belong to one person on the train. It was his father, Boris Baranoff.

Boris Baranoff was a man of great importance during these trying times. Personally selected by Stalin to obtain lend-lease aid from the Americans, Boris was an imposing figure. He was a man whose presence commanded deep respect. He was a tall muscular man with a bristling dark brown moustache and a large protruding nose. His eyebrows were thick with bushy dark brown hair. There was only a little bit of space between the eyebrows. They did not fit his big dark brown eyes that were soft, except when he narrowed them in anger. At those times, his round face could have adorned any poster of an American gangster movie. His gray tunic was a stark and unique contrast to the brown uniforms of the Russian soldiers facing him. Still there was a deep respect from the soldiers for this civilian. They had strict standing orders to obey this man. They stood at rigid attention as he viewed the death scene.

"One of your personal guards has been murdered," stammered one of the soldiers picking up a bloody arm of his fallen comrade. "He has been stabbed."

A nervous looking smaller man from behind Boris spoke up. "Comrade Baranoff, have you seen that dagger? It's a German dagger like the kind their officers use. Some Nazi agent must be on board this train." He nervously scanned the eyes of all the soldiers standing nearby. "Some man who wants to kill you. He could be here right now in this car. Sir, for your own safety, you must not go on to the United States. This assassin was out to get you, not this lazy worm that fell asleep on the job. The Germans obviously know about your mission to obtain lend lease supplies from the Americans. We must turn around at once and go back to Moscow. The mission is already a failure."

Boris angrily turned around to face the meek little aide. "Colonel Jorosky, this so called little worm died trying to protect me. Look at the mess of this room. Comrade Petroloff was a fine man and a martyr in this war against the Nazis menace. Don't ever accuse one of the men on this train of being a coward again or I will personally report you to the Kremlin." Boris glared at the sniveling cowering colonel. "Do I make myself clear?"

"Yes, sir, you do!" came the almost inaudible reply.

Alexander looked up at his father, smiling slightly. He disliked Colonel Jorosky for some reason and was happy when the egotistical man was put into his proper place. The colonel was about to leave when Alexander's father stopped him in his tracks. "Colonel, You know what needs to be done now. Find the treasonous dog that is on this train. I want him found …and I want him to pay for what he has done here. Let me know if there is anyone missing from the train. You have the manifesto of the army personnel on board, so find out quickly who might be gone and we will have our troops scour the countryside behind us. The German pig will not escape so easily. If he is still on the train, then he will have to deal with me." Boris brought up his fists to his waist. "NOW GO FIND THE SWINE!" he bellowed.

Boris kept his narrowing eyes focused on the colonel who had trouble moving. "DISMISSED!"

The colonel brought his chin down to acknowledge the command. He turned to two soldiers standing nearby stretching their necks to view the ghastly scene. "Rondonesleska, Kachenko, remove this body to the baggage car."

The larger man, Corporal Rondoneleska, protested. "Isn't there a better place for him? We can't just leave him in the baggage car like a piece of meat. He deserves better than that."

Jorosky puckered his lips in disgust and glared at his subordinate. "Well, we really don't have too much of a choice until we reach the next refueling depot, do we?" He pointed at the body in anger. "Now do your duty."

Smiling slightly at each other, the two soldiers half-heartily tried to conceal their contempt for the overbearing, pompous Jorosky. Their smiles quickly faded, however, as they set out to perform the grim task of removing their comrade in arms' body to the baggage car.

As the three men carried the limp body down the aisle, Alexander watched the back of their heads. In the dim light of the rail car, Alexander tried to remember what he had seen when he had been alone with the killer. Something suddenly looked familiar as the three soldiers struggled moving the body. The young boy thought about it for a few seconds and then twitched his mouth and figured that it would come back to him later.

Boris turned to his son. "Did you see anything at all?" Alexander didn't respond. He was still trying to figure out what seemed so familiar about one of the three men who were just leaving through the far door.

"Alexander?"

Alexander roused himself and focused on the question that was being asked. "I only saw Private Petroloff's body as I was headed back to the last car to find Private Danipovoroff and him. I did hear the lamp break, however."

Reeling back on what just transpired, the young man frowned at his close call. "It seemed to me that I have always been in the wrong place at the wrong time, Father." Alexander grabbed his father's forearm. His fourteen-year-old body quivered. "Father, I don't want anything to happen to you. They tell me that the assassin was after you, not me."

"That's what I understand as well." Boris scoffed. "Don't worry. It will take more than a sniveling Nazi spy to kill me."

From the back of the crowd that had gathered in the car, one soldier stayed hidden in the shadows. He sneered quietly to himself. "It will not be a sniveling Nazi who will kill you. It will be a brave soldier of the Third Reich who will be honored in Das Deutschland by the Fuehrer himself." He turned to go out to the platform, plotting his next attempt against Boris.

The man narrowed his lips in bitter anger and then grimly smiled. His mind took in the many possibilities of the death of the mediator. "This man is sure to let his guard down sometime and then I will use that opportunity to strike." His thoughts did not reflect what was on his face, but he was determined to kill the man who was trying to obtain weapons that were to be used against his fatherland, Germany. "Comrade Baranoff, I vow I will kill you."

CHAPTER 2

December 6, 1941

Two whole days had passed and nothing more had been revealed about the location of the Nazi infiltrator. With no more immediate undisputable danger, everyone on board the train assumed that the Nazi agent had developed the heart of a coward, fearing that he would soon be discovered. Most of the passengers on the train believed the agent had already jumped off the train to save his own life. Prevailing circumstances added to the assurance that the killer was gone. None of the five men in the last car on the day of the murder had not seen anyone enter their car, and they all had the alibi of being together.

In checking the personnel ledger, Captain Zoronavich had discovered that not all the assigned soldiers were on board the train. One of the other Russian guards had disappeared completely and could not be found anywhere on the train so it was assumed that the missing man was the killer.

Looking throughout the train, it was discovered that one of Comrade Baranoff's guards, Private Zolokov, was the man who was absent. The missing man had been a quiet non-assuming man, but he didn't seem the type to be a killer. Zolokov had constantly been at Boris' side in Leningrad weeks earlier and had plenty of opportunities to kill him. This fact didn't seem to matter to many on board the train.

With Zolokov nowhere to be found on the train, nearly everyone on the board had concluded that he was the German agent who had killed Private Petroloff.

Only Captain Zoronavich had his doubts. Zoronavich would only shake his head when others declared that the killer had departed the train. Besides being a good soldier, Private Zolokov had been a good friend of the captain and he knew the private well. He confided to Boris, "I find it hard to believe that it could be Zolokov. He didn't have that type of personality."

No one listened to the captain's concerns. The tense feelings that had existed earlier had faded somewhat and sporadic tedious fatigue had set in, especially with young Alexander.

In his eagerness to create excitement, Alexander had taken to running up and down the aisle of the railway cars, nearly knocking down a few soldiers in the process. Boris finally had to confine the activities of his enthusiastic son to studies of Marx and Lenin. Alexander objected. "But there is nothing else to do," he protested. "That stuff is so boring."

Boris smirked and shook his head as he rebuked his son. "Be that as it may, we still need to observe the rules of safety on the train. Alexander, I am sorry that there is no one else your age here, but you need to settle down. Get into your studies or find another activity besides running into my soldiers."

"Like what?"

"If you don't want to study, then play chess with someone or begin writing a journal."

"Now father, really! There must be something else I can do."

Boris smiled as he patted Alexander's head. His dark eyes darted towards the back of the car. Despite his gruff exterior, Boris was very loving with his son. "I guess you will find something. Just be careful whatever you do. Don't hurt others around you."

The young teenager pondered alternatives for an activity for a while. Boredom set in quickly for his active mind. Alexander wandered on the aisle of the train compartment trying hard to find something new and different to try.

The rumbling of the train's wheels beneath him made it hard to concentrate on staying awake. The constant rhythm beneath his feet had a calming soothing effect on the boy's mind. He felt safe from the cold world right outside the window even now with the small possibility that a killer still might be on board the train.

As he stared out into the glaring white landscape, Alexander wondered if there was any place on earth that was colder. He could tell by looking at the swirls of the frost-encrusted winds that tumbled around out on the open space that the area right outside the train was bitterly cold. The young Russian had watched the same scene go by ever since he had left Moscow with his father and mother. Alexander now yearned for something other than the constant white blinding snow. The Russian teenager watched the distant horizon, hoping to see a mountain or a city, anything but the same frosty landscape.

The young man wrapped his arms around himself in mock coldness. "Siberia," he thought to himself, "has to be the dreariest place in the world to live. There is nothing out there but snow and that terrible wind. It's no wonder that Premier Stalin sends all the rebellious scoundrels out here. It's the worst punishment that anyone could receive."

"How much different it was here, another place of death?" He had heard rumors of the terrible region called Siberia.

Siberia, a name that even sounded cold and bleak and brought to fear to the common man. It was a place, according to the rumors, of unspeakable labor camps, constant suffering and cold uncalculating death. Siberia was almost as bad as Leningrad in pain and misery. Alexander knew what the rumors said about this place, "Siberia." His own government had made this an area of secret labor camps and cold lingering death was almost as bad, but at least no one was purposely trying to kill anyone here, at least not inside of the train.

Alexander, along with many others on the train, had heard about the harsh penalties and alleged atrocities from the local inhabitants. Everywhere the train had stopped in Siberia, the local inhabitants quietly described the labor camps in the surrounding areas. There had been no dignity or fondness in what they had seen.

Despite the long tedious trip the young man was enduring, he knew in his heart that there were definitely worse places to be in the world, even in other parts of his own country. The harsh realities of war had practically taken over the entire eastern European area. Moscow itself was being threatened by the Nazis. Leningrad was in danger of falling to the German war machine.

Holding out against overwhelming odds, the Russians in Leningrad were near collapse. Most military experts in Moscow and Berlin expected the city to surrender at any time. There was a constant barrage of German artillery and the Luftwaffe had free reign in the air above to bomb the frozen city at will. The people of Leningrad were dying by the hundreds as they succumbed to starvation, disease, cold, and the Nazi artillery.

Despite the sobering reality of the suffering in Leningrad, Alexander could not understand the reason for this journey. What was so important about the secret mission that his father was supposed to accomplish in a far away land called America? All he knew about his father's mission was that it had something to do with the borrowing of weapons and the words "lend-lease". He had asked questions before, but he always wanted to know more. The boy wandered back to where his father was working on a report.

Alexander could see that his father was in deep thought, but decided to ask the questions that had been bothering him for the last fifty miles. "Father, why do we depend on the Americans for our weapons?"

Boris looked at his son with an endearing smile. The big man with the tender heart could understand and appreciate his son's inquisitive spirit. He had learned from experience that the boy would often question his father about such things. Boris actually appreciated the chance to teach his son about life. The cherished time spent with his son and answering his questions brought the two closer together.

Boris rubbed his chin and shifted his eyes out towards the distant horizon outside to consider an answer. His moustache twitched in an up and down motion. After a brief respite, he answered. "You know that the Russians do not need to fear anyone in the world for we have the strongest army in the world and our people have the intrinsic and true spirit to overcome anything."

Alexander nodded his head in acknowledgment.

"And you know that we are fighting the Germans who will stop at nothing until the Russian people are dead as a nation."

Alexander nodded head again, but with a slow methodical bobbing motion that indicated questioning.

"This madman, this self-made demagogue who became the Judas goat of the German sheep, he has the gall to say that the German people are part of the master Aryan race and that they should control the world. Do you want to know the truth? The Germans are nothing more than arrogant puppets! They are being led like lambs to the slaughter by this...this dictator, Adolph Hitler. He is a dangerous lunatic and he must be stopped at all costs." Boris banged his fist into his opened palm, remembering the people who had died at his beloved Leningrad.

Boris glared at Alexander and continued his speech with a serious tone. "It is imperative that such atrocities as what this evil man is creating be stopped. We only accept weapons from the Americans to insure that the Nazis are defeated completely and soundly."

With a softer flush of color in his face, Boris put his hand on Alexander's shoulder. He could tell by his son's eyes that he still did not understand completely. He vaguely remembered the time when he too was so innocent and full of questions that lacked clear answers from his parents.

Alexander looked puzzled. "This may all be true, but on top of what you just told me, you constantly remind me that the Americans despise us. Doesn't that make you wonder about the integrity of the American people? They must be helping us for some reason. I could understand if they let us fight it out with the Germans so that we both would be weakened, but it seems like they really want us to win."

Boris scoffed at the very notion of what his son was implying. "The Americans are only looking out for themselves. They truly believe that if Hitler could beat us and push his way completely through our country, he would attack America through Alaska and Canada. That is the only reason they are helping us."

Trying a new approach, Boris twisted his lips in order to bring out the real reason for American aid. "Alexander, the Soviet Union does have its limitations, even if we are the greatest nation on earth. The aid we receive from the Americans will help us defeat the Nazis so they will never endanger our country again. Hitler is unorthodox in the way he fights his battles. There is always the small possibility that he could find a weak point somewhere along our front lines and exploit it. That is why we must take every measure to make sure that he will not be able to take the advantage. Soon the Germans will be forced to fight the Americans as well as the English and us. If it takes till the crack of doomsday to destroy Hitler, we will do it."

Boris leaned back from his teaching posture. "With the Americans helping, it will go that much quicker. The only way we can fight on forever with our limited resources is to use other provisional possibilities for our supply needs. Our country has just so much to offer. We sometimes have to look elsewhere for other measures to shorten our suffering. One of these measures is the war supplies from the United States. The British have been quite successful against the Germans since their acceptance of lend-lease aid. If they can do it with the aid of the Americans, then why can't we? Any help can only mean the quickest defeat of Hitler." Boris tipped his head in an inquiring manner as his eye brows raised up to see if the boy understood completely what his father was trying to teach him.

Alexander laid his chin into the arch of his thumb and index finger. "I wonder what America will be like?" The young boy's eyes glistened in questioning wonder.

Boris gave his son a cocky and insignificant look and his lips curled downwards. "Don't expect too much from those people. They will be very different from the people that we know in Moscow and Leningrad. You have to be careful around them. They are untrustworthy and they hate our illustrious communist system of governing. The only reason that I am bringing you along to be among these corruptible capitalists is that I would worry about you back in Leningrad." Boris cleared his throat and enhanced his previous statement. "And I want you and your mother to be by me as well. I would miss both of you very much if I were in America by myself. To tell you the truth, I want to be with you forever if I could."

Alexander smiled and nodded his head. He was positive that he had heard the right answer. The most important aspect he heard was that his father cared.

Boris grinned and his belly shook. "The Americans may not have what we want." In a sarcastically half-serious pretentious scowl, Boris teased his son. "Well, we'll see what the Americans have to offer us anyway."

Boris turned to go to the dining car. "Remember Alexander, the weapons of an adversary can be used just as effectively against him as it can against the enemy or an untrusting benefactor."

CHAPTER 3

Despite the warnings that his father had given him about the shortcomings of America, Alexander knew from his experience in Leningrad that the United States had to have some good qualities. The main reason, of course, in Alexander's mind was there was no war there. His thoughts drifted once again to his hometown, a city that was in shambles because of the Germans. Men, women, and children were being sacrificed daily in the city.

Alexander understood all too well that Hitler had to be completely defeated. He knew that in order to destroy Hitler, compromises had to be made with the Americans.

His father had explained to him that the United States was afraid that Hitler would eventually sweep through the Soviet Union with his army. If that were to happen, it was assumed by the Americans that Hitler's next step would be to invade the United States, slicing through Alaska and Canada.

One of the lend-lease mediators for the Russians was Alexander's father, Boris Baranoff.

Even though Boris was against the principles of the United States, he was in complete compliance with his superiors for arranging for these capitalistic supplies.

His one concern was for his family. Boris had asked permission of the Premier to take his family with him to America. This request was granted because the Premier needed the mediator to concentrate solely on war supplies and not on his family who might have been left behind in a war zone.

Boris understood completely that his hometown of Leningrad would be one of the first places that the Nazis would attack in the Soviet Union. He had hoped that his wife and son would be able to come with him out of harm's way. Thinking of the present circumstances, Alexander Baranoff was happy to be on board a train bound for the seaport city of Vladivostok.

With the war going on in Europe and Russia, Alexander was anxious to get as far away as the train would take him from the western regions of the Soviet Union. In a way, he felt somewhat guilty as being one of the few to escape the war-torn region where many of his friends and relatives were struggling to stay alive. He would often wonder, "Was it much different from where he was now in the eastern part of the Soviet Union?"

Alexander, with his father's help, slowly recognized the fact that the Germans had to be defeated at any cost, even if it meant cooperating with the Americans. This was the compromise that couldn't be avoided if the Soviet Union was to stay in the war.

Historical events had shown him that his father was right. The dictator Hitler was a madman. He proved that after he betrayed the Russians and had attacked them earlier that year. Hadn't the German leader signed a non-aggression treaty with the Russians in August of 1939? He had even lied to the then Prime Minister, Neville Chamberlain of England. What good was the man's word? He was not to be trusted anywhere. What if this crazy individual was able to gain access to a destructive weapon that would enable him to destroy the world?

Alexander understood too well by watching his friends die in Leningrad that Hitler had to be destroyed.

With Hitler's constant victories lately, Alexander recognized the cold hard fact that the Soviet Union was in real danger. The Germans had swept through every country that they had attacked already, with the exception of the Soviet Union and England. Stalin would take no chances and had reluctantly agreed to lend-lease aid from America. At least that is what Alexander had been told by his father.

But now there were persistent questions that entered Alexander's mind. He was sure that somehow, the entire truth was hidden from him by his parents and teachers. There were faint rumors that Stalin was persecuting his own people, even though no one would whisper it out loud. There were atrocities being committed by his own leader to invoke fear and trepidation.

Stalin was not a man to be trifled with and many who did paid for it with their lives. Such accusations of the harshness of the labor camps would prove to be dangerous during these times, possibly even fatal.

For all his supposed faults, Stalin did have his good side though. Many friends and high officials believed strongly that he made the right decision when he picked Boris Baranoff for ambassador for lend-lease aid. He had personally appointed Boris Baranoff for this dangerous assignment. Through all the turmoil of leaving home, Boris was grateful to Stalin and more than happy that his wife and son would be able to come with him. With this type of reward, Boris would serve to the death in loyalty to the dictator of the Soviet Union.

Boris and his family had several difficulties leaving Leningrad when they did. The city had been almost been completely encircled by the invading Germans. Starvation was almost as deadly as the enemy. The harsh winter snows had been bitterly cold. The weather had been hard on communications. With little information, most of the world had come to the conclusion that the ancient northern capital of Russia would fall at any time. This pessimistic attitude included many Russians as well.

The danger of the Germans encircling Leningrad at any time was a very strong possibility during the early winter of 1941. The Baranoff family had escaped just in time.

Safely past the German lines, Boris Baranoff and his family made their way to Moscow. There had been rumors that the Germans had infiltrated an agent along the route, but no one took the threat seriously. They believed that strict Soviet security regulations would take care of any possibility of a German agent.

From Moscow, the Baranoffs had taken a train east on the Trans-Siberian railway. The route that the Baranoff family was taking to America would be across the Siberian plains to Vladivostok. From there they would take a ship to Tokyo. Then if all went according to the pre-made arrangements, the plan was to sail on from Tokyo to San Francisco.

Boris wasn't quite sure that this would be the best way to travel. There were strong indications that in a short while, there would be no traffic between Japan and America.

Boris himself had strong suspicions because of recent events, known even in the highest echelons of his own country. Stalin had already begun to remove troops from the eastern shores of the Soviet Union. Why else would he do this unless he knew personally that the Japanese had made concessions towards the Russian Premier? Boris mentioned to his aide, Zonronavich, "I'm afraid we may be headed to an even bigger hornet's nest. The trouble is that we just don't know which way certain countries will head to in the direction of war. The Japanese are masters of deception. They can easily hide their motives from anyone."

The aide nodded. "I agree, sir, but we have a mission to complete, no matter which direction the Japanese government takes."

Boris nodded in agreement. "I know that we are uneasy partners with the Americans, but we do need the aid. What makes it real hard to deal with them is the fact that we have not joined their embargo against the Japanese. I wonder how much longer the Japanese government will tolerate that arrangement." He puckered his lips in a perplexed display. "I must admit that they are generous with their lend-lease weapons and this may last only until the end of the war."

Boris was determined in his resolve to succeed in his mission. "I hope it continues in any case. They must continue. I must not fail in my endeavor. I do not wish to see any more dead Russians. We must all accomplish our goal."

Boris Baranoff had a strong suspicion that Premier Stalin already knew where the Japanese would strike next, and it wouldn't be the Soviet Union. More than likely, the Premier knew that the Japanese had decided that attacking the Soviet Union was not in their best interests. As strong as their war party and their war expansionist policy had become, Japan was expected to attack someone else soon. If not the Russians, than who?

Boris assumed that the Japanese would attack somewhere else as well. It made sense. In his talks with the consulate, Boris assumed that the Japanese people needed large amounts of raw materials and oil to continue their war with China. The Japanese consultant had tipped off by his actions, a certain direction of his country's ambitions. He was trying to get reassurances of the Soviet Union's non-aggression stance just in case the Japanese went to war. Boris assumed the worst for those countries that had colonies in the oil rich regions of the South Pacific. These colonial powers included the Netherlands, France, Great Britain, and of course, the United States. How safe were the Philippines? After all, the Japanese needed large amounts of raw material and oil to continue their war with China. The Russians and the Japanese both knew that attacking the Soviet Union would not be the easiest way to gain these much-needed supplies. It would be absolutely ridiculous to capture the oil fields of the Caucus region of Russia. They were located too far into the interior of that country. The only other recourse was to obtain the materials they needed through a closer source.

The only other recourse was to obtain the raw material and oil from another possible source, which meant taking another path of action. If not north to the Soviet Union, then the only other way was to the south. That meant a head on collision with either the British or the Americans.

Boris Baranoff had a good idea what might happen to the United States. Despite the unannounced and ongoing sea battles between the Nazis and the United States, the Germans were not their most immediate threat. Major politicians had secretly confided in Boris because of his anti-American stance. They had told him that their intelligent reports from their agent in Tokyo had confirmed that the Japanese were ready to drive south instead of north.

For the moment, Boris didn't worry too much about relations between the Americans and the Japanese. His main concern was getting the war materials to fight the Germans. The Nazi war machine lately had seemed unstoppable. The Germans had swept over most of the western frontier of the Soviet Union and were even threatening the great capital of Moscow itself. Boris knew that his people in the western part of the Soviet Union were in for a hard struggle. There would be many lives lost even though he believed that the Russians were the strongest people on the earth. "Even the strong die eventually." Boris mumbled in reluctant realization. There were daily reports and rumors coming from the west that his own city of Leningrad was near collapse and was one of the cities that was the hardest hit of all of the major Russian cities. Boris thought about all his relatives and friends that he had left behind. There was the strongest feeling in his heart that many of his loved ones would be dead and gone by the time he returned. His heart ached for the struggle for life many of his family and friends were going through in their fight for their very existence. He yearned to make sure that he could continue his fight in the best way he knew how by getting the lend-lease weapons.

Before starting the trip to the east, Boris had been informed that the Germans might have some information on his mission and that there would probably be some attempt from the Nazis to stop him from completing it. Boris was skeptical and informed his security people that the Germans would never try anything this far into Soviet territory. Still, he worried more for his fellow Russians than he did for himself.

At least his wife and son were with him. This was a reassuring comforting thought in itself.

His young son, Alexander, was also looking forward to getting out of the Soviet Union, especially the western region where the fighting had been fierce. It was a war-torn area where many friends and relatives were struggling to stay alive.

Nevertheless, Alexander wished that he could see something other than the vast white plains of Siberia. The scenery was monotonous and bleak. There was nothing else to do but talk to the soldiers or sleep, neither of which was all that exciting.

Alexander thought long and hard. He was anxious to see a new country, even if it belonged to the people who despise the communist government. Alexander constantly wondered what the Americans were really like and why they weren't helping the Germans instead of helping the Soviet people.

As Alexander shook his head at the cold world outside of the train, he wondered if America would be any better than his own homeland. He had considerable doubts because of what his father had taught him about Americans. His education system had also taught him that Americans were evil capitalists eventually bent on the destruction of the soviet system of government.

His father had warned him many times that he could never trust a capitalist Yankee. "All they ever think about is how to become richer and fatter, feeling superior to the rest of the world because of all of their wealth. They are weak-minded idiots who have terribly misguided moral values. For the time being however they are not our main concern. There are some on board the train, including my chief of staff, who are more concerned with rumors of spies and as-sassins."

"It is still a possibility," Zoronavich warned.

"There is no spy on board." scoffed Boris as he slapped both of his knees. "We need to think about getting to the United States."

"That's not what has me concerned!" stated his second in com-mand, Lt. Vladimir Zaronavich. "True, they may try no large scale attack on this train, but if your mission is known to the German high command, they may consider it important enough to send another saboteur to stop you."

"Poppy cock!" Boris rebuked him. "Unless our security is vul-nerable in eastern Russia, we have nothing to fear."

Sonja, his wife, was not so optimistic. With an imploring look of concern, she tried to convince her husband that more precaution should be taken. "My dear husband, maybe you should listen to the lieutenant. Out here in the middle of nowhere is the most likely place for a German spy to strike."

Boris gruffly and skeptically wrinkled his mouth. "Do what you wish," he told Vladimir, "but I want no delays or interference with my operation. Is that clear?" he growled indicating a warning.

"Yes sir!" Vladimir nervously replied. He glanced over to Sonja who nodded in quick agreement. She was happy that Boris would give his okay to some protection. After all, she loved him very much and didn't want any harm to come to him. They were far away from the war, but danger still loomed large as far as she was concerned. It was not worth the risk to let him go unprotected.

Later that night

The initial investigation by Lieutenant Zaronavich had come to the conclusion that everyone had an alibi when the murder occurred except one man. The verification was only brought out after all the men were accounted for fifteen minutes after the murder. "Anyone could have slipped into the ranks of men during that time." Everyone had been accounted for except Private Zolokov. Zolokov was still the main suspect, largely due to the fact that he was nowhere to be found.

Zaronavich continued to have some doubts. He assumed that the Nazi spy was still on the train. Zaronavich concurred with Boris that the killer might have doubled back after being discovered by Alexander thus throwing suspicion off himself. "This man, this Nazi is clever. We should watch our steps. The killer more than likely went forward and was passed by during the search."

Soon, everyone found out how devious and cunning the hunted individual could be. They also found out how merciless and cruel the spy could be as the train stopped at the next station. The news would raise new fears.

Lieutenant Daipavoroff nervously entered the stateroom where Boris was working on his reports. "Comrade, the murderer is still on board the train. The 38th militia near Polentestska has just telegraphed. They have informed us that Private Zolokov's body was found near the tracks 450 kilometers west of here. His throat had been cut. He could not have been the spy we have been looking for. Sir, your life is still in danger!" Panic filled his voice.

Boris stroked his beard and glared at Daipavoroff. He did not want to invoke any more fear from Sonja. Bravely he stated, "I suggest then that you find the killer and dispose of him. I'm going to work out the logistics of the lend-lease program, and I want to make it plain that no one is to bother me. I'll be in my stateroom."

Boris turned to go to his room and Sonja slowly followed him. She was afraid for her husband's life, but she understood that these were dangerous times. She would stand by him no matter what. "Boris, you must take these men seriously. Do not make yourself visible. You must not make yourself a moving target. Stay in your room until they find him."

Boris squinted with his left eye at Sonja in defiance. "That's nonsense! My men will catch him."

He could see the fear in her face. He patted her arm. "If you insist."

"I do."

He strolled towards his stateroom. Sonja shook her head. "What about a guard?"

"Until I find out who the Nazi is, I can't trust any guard. I'll be okay," he tried to reassure her.

Now with the evidence of the dead army private, it was plain to see that a Nazi killer was still on board the train and he was trying his best to stop Boris from reaching the United States. It was equally clear that the killer was smart and devious.

It was three hours later when Alexander slipped out of bed and stumbled half awake into the narrow aisle of the moving train. Some odd noise had aroused him from his slumber. He tried to shake the sleep from his eyes so he could focus on where he was going.

Turning the corner at the end passageway, Alexander could barely see that his father's light in the room next door was still on. Alexander slipped on his bathrobe and walked out into the passageway of the rail car. The light inside the reddish-brown hallway was dim, but it was light enough for Alexander to barely see his way to the washroom.

Alexander stepped momentarily outside his door as he heard a muffled noise down at the other end of the narrow hallway. It was a heavy breathing sound of fear and recluse. He peered through the dimly lit rail car, but could see nothing at the other end. He continued to the washroom.

The constant clacking of the wheels beneath him was a sooth-ing noise, but Alexander was still bothered by the noise that he had heard earlier. It wasn't the usual noise of the train. Alexander decid-ed to go back to his room and see what the unexplained disturbance could be. As he started around the corner from the washroom, he suddenly noticed the glint of steel in the hallway near his parents' stateroom. A dark figure was crouched near the doorway as if try-ing to look under the drawn curtain of the room. Alexander watched horrified as the shiny object, a gun, was being raised and pointed towards the occupants of the room. Alexander's instincts instantly took over as he raised his cupped left hand to his mouth.

CHAPTER 4

Alexander recognized right away that the gun was aimed straight at his father. A sudden burst of light from the outside moon swept the face of the assassin. It was Jorosky's aide-de-camp, Corporal Ivan Rondonesleska. Even with the brief light, Alexander could see the twisted and hard-lined scowl of Rondonesleska. The Nazi's face was full of hatred.

Alexander opened his mouth in stunned recognition. Rondonesleska was clearly the Nazi spy that the Soviet Council had warned Boris to watch out for and avoid.

Without giving his own position any consideration or concern, Alexander immediately yelled out, "Hey Nazi!" hoping to distract Rondenesleska, who was posed to shoot.

Startled, Rondenesleska wheeled immediately towards the boy. With a semi-lightning reflex, the Nazi agent quickly leveled his lugar at the boy and fired his weapon.

Alexander fortunately was a second faster than his would be executioner and was positioned near the corner of the passenger car hallway. He lunged around the corner just as the shot ranged out. The bullet splintered the oak joint of the support beam.

Alexander felt a series of jolts in his back and quickly reached for his spinal column. There was a small amount of blood on his palm. Small fragments of wood had embedded into Alexander's back, a result of the splintering of the oak beam that had been hit by the deadly projectile.

Irritated by the disruption of his aim, Rondonesleska started after the young teenager to get revenge for being discovered. He halted momentarily and decided that Boris was a more important target. He turned and ran back to the closed stateroom door.

Boris, awakened by the Alexander's yell, had been able to push his wife into the closet, just as the German agent had turned to fire at Alexander.

Rondonesleska, in his frustration, squatted at the opening of Boris and Sonja's stateroom and tried to fire open the lock of the door. Sonja screamed on hearing the blast. The Nazi knew now where she was located.

Bending low on his knee, the infuriated Nazi agent looked through the partially drawn curtains. It was at that split second that he could see activity inside the stateroom. Boris was diving under the bed for cover.

Rondonesleska pointed his lugar at the bed and knew that the mattresses would not be able to save Boris from being killed. Once completing his task, Rondonesleska's next bullet would be aimed at the wife of his sworn enemy. It was a certainty that Sonja would not be safe in the closet from her impending death.

Shots rang out from the far end of the railway car and the Nazi agent jerked backwards and slumped to the floor in a half-sitting position. The sudden impact of Soviet bullets ensured that Rondonesleska was unable to fire off his shot. Blood flowed freely out of a dime-sized hole near his stomach and the German reached down to see if it was really his blood. The dizziness in his head confirmed that it was his own life giving fluid. He looked up to see three Russian soldiers pointing their rifles at him. The ends of the barrels were still smoking.

"Prekratit' strel' bu!" (Hold your fire!), came a nearby, but frantic command.

One of the Russian guards ran up to the crumpling German and kicked the lugar away from out of his hand. Rondonesleska laughed at this gesture for he knew that he didn't have the strength to lift the pistol. A second sudden pain gripped the man in the side and Rondoneleska knew he was dying.

Boris tied a silk cord around his nightshirt and unlatched the lock to his stateroom. He came out and stood over his would-be executioner.

The smell of fresh gunpowder permeated the stale air in the rail-road car. A residue of gray smoke still laced the ceiling.

In stunned agitation, Boris constricted his fist and put it in the palm of his other hand. He glared momentarily at the traitor and bent down beside him.

The Russian guards continued to point their rifles at the German agent. Fearing for the ambassador, the soldiers were adamant with Boris and stated their objections. "He could still be dangerous!" as they warned Boris to stay away from Rondonesleska, but Boris waved their protests aside.

The German agent coughed as he noticed his would-be victim sitting by him. Blood was running out of the corners of his mouth. "You Russian coward, the Fuehrer knows of your plan to obtain war materials from the United States. We know as well you will try to bring this illegal booty by way of the Pacific passage at Vladivostok." Rondonesleska wavered for a moment, his voice growing weaker. "You will have no more success out there than you did when your weapons were brought in by way of the Atlantic Ocean. Our Japanese allies will stop you from bringing war materials into Eastern Siberia. They will stop you in your evil scheme." He struggled briefly for breath. "Remember this: the Japanese will destroy the weak-minded Americans. As a people, Americans have no stomach for war. If Russia sides with them, it will make you weaker. These foolish Americans will retreat as soon as they enter the war. You won't be able to get one rifle from them." The German's eyes faded away briefly then opened wide. He was beginning to lose consciousness. "The Americans don't trust you. They won't give you something for nothing. In fact, they won't give you a thing."

Boris grabbed the dying man's head. "One thing that we have going for us, they trust that madman Hitler even less."

Rondonesleska grimaced to hear his Fueher's name associated with being a madman. His eyes fluttered in a death grip. Boris let go of the spy's head and it dropped with a dull thud on the floor of the rail car. One last gasp came from the Nazi and he was dead.

Grimacing in pain and holding his shoulder, Alexander, standing in the near corner of the car, glanced uneasily at the dead agent. Rondonesleska's expressionless eyes were blankly staring up to the ceiling.

Boris looked down at the dead man and turned the corners of his mouth down in disgust. "So be it to all traitorous dogs."

Glancing up, Boris eyes moistened. "For you, Privates Zolovov and Petroloff." Boris smiled as he faced his son, who was just standing up from his position around the corner of the hallway. "Did you yell at him just as he was about to shoot me?"

Alexander was shaking. "Yes, sir!"

Boris nodded his head once. "I believed so much that we would avoid any trouble with the Germans out here, but it wasn't possible I see." Suddenly, Boris' expression turned sour as he stepped over the dead man's body to be closer to his son. "And what were you trying to do? Kill yourself? That was idiotic to put your life in danger like that. If that man would have killed you, there would be no reason for my existence. Don't you ever try something like that again! Do I make myself clear?"

Alexander looked down at the floor and stammered as he answered his father. "Yes, sir, I do!"

Boris smiled once more and spoke in a softer tone. "Still, you were a brave lad. A little headstrong at times, but a brave lad nevertheless, thank you." He reemphasized his position on the matter. "…but don't ever put your life on the line for my sake ever again."

Boris put his palm against Alexander's shoulder. As he withdrew his hand, Boris suddenly noticed the red holes in Alexander's shirt and the blood on his palm. "Alexander, are you all right?"

Alexander flinched as he felt the sting on his back as his father touched the small wound. "I'm fine, Father. I just had a small run in with some wood splinters. They don't hurt too much."

Boris grabbed his son and turned him to look at the wounds on his back. "Wood splinters can cause infection." He ushered his son to a nearby wash basin. "Let's go in here and clean them up. We'll put a clean dressing on it as well."

Zoronavich, the adjutant to Boris, looked down at the body of

Rondonesleska and put his hands up to his hips. He glowered at the soldiers that had just run in from the other railway car and were standing around, dumbfounded. "Get this...this body out of here. At our next stop, dump it out beside the track and burn it. Leave no trace of his rotting carcass around to tarnish our sacred soil."

The guards responded immediately and started dragging the body out to the baggage car. Fresh blood streaked across the floor where the body had been towed.

Lieutenant Jorosky turned to his superior. "Doesn't this convince you, Comrade? The Germans definitely know who you are and what your mission is and where you are going. We must cancel the rest of the operation. They will probably risk sending someone else."

Boris had enough of the pompous junior officer. "You want to turn and run because of one dead German." Boris glared at his second in command. "Don't be absurd! There are people dying in my own city of Leningrad because they don't have enough weapons to fight with. No! I am not going to let them down because I was almost assassinated by one incompetent spy. No, my friend, this mission is much too important. We must obtain the war materials from the Americans and that is my main objective, first and overall. It is much too important to the lives of my countrymen that I succeed in this task or it is possible that our country will fall into the hands of the Germans. I am going on! Besides, they won't try to send someone this far into Russia. They know we will be on our guard now."

Boris looked at his son and then back at his adjutant. "It is for the future of the Soviet people, if nothing else."

Alexander gently smiled at his father as if he understood. Privately he thought, *What kind of future will we have? Are these dangers only here or are they in America as well?*

Boris restated his position again in a low but gruff voice. "We are still going to America, Colonel."

Jorosky looked down in dejection. "If that is your choice."

Boris puffed up his chest in one slow methodical breath. "Colonel, I want you to understand that Rondenesleska was your responsibility. Were you not the one who signed him up for duty on this train? We must not let this oversight happen again. I am sending you back to Moscow on the next train west. Maybe you will be in a position back on the front line where you will be more responsible. You are dismissed."

Jorosky opened his mouth as if to reply, but he quickly saluted and turned away and left.

Alexander slowly sat down on a nearby stall. He was feeling weary from all of the excitement that had happened. His mind felt tortured and he had learned to grow wary of events that could possibly be forthcoming for the future. There had been too much killing for him, even for the short time of his life. He whispered to himself. "My world has been almost nothing but despair. Can I ever be in a place that no one wants to kill anyone else? This country of America—Father tells me that there is no war there. America must be close to being the most extraordinary place in the world, if they have no war." Alexander sighed in thinking such phenomenal and unimaginable thoughts. "I wonder, though, if they too don't have some problems that I don't know about yet."

His mother sighed. "I hope not. There has to be peace somewhere in this world. I do hope so for your sake."

CHAPTER 5

December 8, 1941

"White, white, white—nothing but white everywhere you look. When will it ever end?" Alexander fumed with gritted teeth as the perpetual winter scene passed outside the moving train. The young man gazed impatiently out unto the vast frosty wilderness of the Siberian frontier that was passing by in an apparently redundant and repetitive terrain. "It looks so cold out there, nothing but snow for miles around!"

If it wasn't bad enough, the freezing temperatures were not confined just to the outside in the taiga of the frozen plain. It was hardly better inside the passenger car of the train.

Alexander blew warm air on the window and his breath instantly turned into a misty covering of frost on the window pane. Unable to concentrate on anything else but the snow, Alexander eventually sank down lower into his blanket that he had cuddled up into for warmth and closed his eyes. He believed that the only good useful purpose that he could see for this snowbound place was the fact that the war, for the most part, seemed distant. It was a relief to know that no one in a gray uniform with a swastika was around trying to butcher you. It was difficult for Alexander to remember that it was only the day before when deception and fear had come not from the gray uniform of a German soldier, but under the mask of a trusted Russian officer.

The German, Rondonesleska, was dead. Alexander still shuddered as he thought how close his entire family had come to death.

"The Nazis could only be out here under a coward's disguise." Alexander cringed at the thought of the former killer, Rondonesleska. "Up to that point, I considered this place to be safe from all of the slaughter. Until that German murderer came along, no one was purposely trying to kill anyone out here. Why had Rondonesleska tried to kill my father? Why had that terrible man brought the war out to Siberia? Why do men have to kill each other in the first place?" Alexander muddled his thoughts briefly and considered where he was headed. "Will America be a land where everyone is fighting too? Could it possibly be the only place in the world where people get along with each other—or will they get involved in the war too?"

"America." The young man sank down into his seat and focused on the snowy plains outside of the window. "Will the weather be like this in the United States? Oh, I wish I could see something else besides death and snow." Alexander wanted to please his father and be complacent about his present situation, but the memories of his war–ravaged home and Rondonesleaka were too vivid.

Alexander turned to his father. "The place where we are going in the United States, will it be like this, I mean as far as the weather goes?"

Boris smiled. "No, the place we are headed to is called California. It is supposed to be quite warm there with hardly any snow." Boris looked out to gaze at the scenery. "From Vladivostok to Toyko, then we sail on to a city in this California called San Francisco."

Alexander was quite pleased with the description of the destination. He was hoping with all of his heart that he would soon see something other than the vast white plains. Alexander had to admit that it was becoming quite boring here on the train and he was anxious to see other lands, even if it was going to be the government of one of his country's adversaries.

As Alexander shook his head at the cold world outside of the train, he wondered if the United States would be any better than the harsh reality of his own homeland. He had considerable doubts, because of what his father had taught him about Americans.

If what Alexander's father had been telling him about America was not enough, the same information was taught to him through the Russian schools. The Soviet education system had taught the young man early on that Americans were evil capitalists whose main goal was the destruction of the Soviet system of government.

Back in Leningrad, Alexander's father consistently warned him, "Never trust a Yankee capitalist. All they ever want to do is to become richer at the expense of other people. Overall, they are fatter than most people of the world because of this exploitation. They are a depraved people with few moral values. The major reason the Americans think they are superior to the rest of the world is because of their vast wealth. In reality, they are weak-minded idiots who have terribly misguided standards of life."

Retreating to a nearby bench near a frosty window, Alexander considered his father's distrust of American capitalists and his philosophy of life.

Few individuals on the train could truly see what Alexander had known all his life about his father. Boris Baranoff was a truly good man. It was his physical appearance that made him look more intimidating than he actually was in real life. He was large and strong with an overbearing voice that seems to shake the roof when he yelled. Few people could see, however, the gentle side of this man and the love that he displayed continuously for his family. The man was a paradox in his treatment of different individuals.

His mother was a gentle soul, even more than his dad. She had soft features that made her the complete opposite of her husband. She constantly had a smile that reflected in her eyes. She always knew how to bring happiness to Alexander, even in the toughest situations. She was not a beautiful woman for the most part, but her kindness was a type of beauty all by itself. It was she who comforted Alexander and knew when he needed guidance and advice. She continuously had a twinkling smile in her eyes that perked Alexander up when he was frightened or alone. She always seemed to know what he was thinking. Even now, she gazed at him knowing somehow that he needed someone to talk to besides all the well meaning, but uninteresting adults on this train. "Do you miss people your own age?" she asked with bright inquisitive eyes.

"Yeah, sort of," he replied quietly.

Sonja grabbed him by the nose and gently shook it. "I know you, my little pertriska. Maybe you will meet a nice girl out here in the snow that is just right for you."

Alexander shyly grinned. "Mama, you have me all wrong. I never think about girls, not with you around."

His mother looked at him with loving doubt in her eyes, and then she smiled.

They both laughed as she embraced him.

It was at that moment the train began to slow down. There was a sudden jerk backwards for the people on board and as they stood up and adjusted to the gradual slowing down of the train.

Boris realized that something was wrong because the train was not scheduled to stop along the way. The ambassador's face etched slowly into a mask of anger as he twisted his head slowly around, looking for a scapegoat to take the brunt of his impatience.

There was a knock at the door of the stateroom where Boris and Sonja had been talking to their son.

"Enter!" Boris halfway shouted.

The brakeman of the engine came in.

"Why are we slowing down?" Boris verbally and impatiently berated the man. "There were to be no stops between Moscow and Vladivostok!" He exchanged a glance towards Zoronavich.

"I understand that you are on an important mission, Comrade Baranoff, but there is an urgent signal coming from the next station ahead of us. They are telling us to stop. Sir, we have no choice. The signal must not be ignored. There may be trouble on the tracks ahead. Remember our predicament, sir. The Nazis now know about your mission. The rail lines ahead could be mined."

"Very well, but this better be important. We need no more delays! Every hour we sit here means another dead Russian at the front! We need to reach our destination as soon as we can." He turned towards his wife and motioned to her with a beckoning finger. "Let's see what is going on."

Boris began to exit towards the vestibule, but he paused to look out the window. "Where are we anyway?"

"Chernyshevsk," the brakeman replied. "We are not that far from the Macchukoo border! The Japanese outposts are just beyond those hills."

"The Chinese border. What do you think? The Japanese wouldn't try anything here."

The brakeman shrugged his shoulders. "Everyone knows that it wasn't all that long ago that the Japanese had signed a treaty with the Nazis." He looked at Boris with concern. "Do you suppose that they have just declared war on us? If they did, we're in a bad place here. We have no support for miles around!"

Boris shook his head. "You never know, but I really believe that we're not the ones to worry."

Boris walked with the brakeman to the head of the passenger compartment where a Soviet army official was standing with two aides.

Boris approached the official sharply and made it clear that he was in no mood to wait for an explanation. "What is the meaning of holding up this train? I'm on a vital mission for Premier Stalin."

The army official stammered. "We understand your mission, sir, but the Soviet supreme command in Moscow instructed me to issue you a new order. It is imperative that you to alter your course. New transportation is being arranged for you at the military air base outside of Irkutsk. A military air transport will take you and your family to Vladivostok, where you will catch a flight to Nome, Alaska. All negotiations with the Americans will be conducted from there. You are not to take a ship to America."

Boris glared at the official. He knew that this sudden change would cause unwarranted delays that would cost the lives of his people fighting in the west. Boris definitely believed with all his heart that the Germans would win more territory if they were not stopped soon. Boris, with anger in his voice and a red face, demanded an explanation. "What nincompoop ordered these changes to be made? It is impossible to obey such a command. I mean, it doesn't make sense. What possible reason could there be for going to Alaska instead of San Francisco as we had planned?" Boris was so enraged that the army official cowered and glanced nervously at his aide. He frowned at the unpleasantness of the situation and turned back to face Boris.

"The orders came in from our top intelligent department. Due to recent events, it will be impossible for you to travel by boat to America."

Boris glared at the official and demanded, "What events would prevent me from going to San Francisco?"

There was an uneasy pause. "Well, tell me!" Boris scowled.

The official sighed. "As of three hours ago, the United States of America and the Empire of Japan have been at war. If you were to board a ship bound for America, Japanese warships would, more than likely, force you to turn around. Even worse, they could sink the ship you were supposed to be on. The whole Pacific Ocean is presently one huge battlefield."

Boris Baranoff gasped in shocked amazement, even though he had his suspicions that war might be a major possibility between the Orientals and the Caucasians. "Japan, America, at war! When did all this happen and where? How did it begin?"

The official cocked his head slightly and glanced at the southeastern horizon. "The Imperial Japanese Naval Forces just attacked the largest American naval base in Hawaii. There was significant damage to the American ships."

Boris scratched the bottom of his chin with his index finger.

His adjutant, Zonronavich, cleared his throat and dared to utter the words that Rondonesleska had relayed to Boris before he died. "That means that it may not be safe for this entourage to go on to America. Maybe we should think about going back?"

Boris thought about what this would mean if he didn't continue with his mission. He wanted to make it perfectly clear to everyone within earshot what his immediate plans were going to be. "Without the supplies from the United States, the Union of Soviet Socialist Republics could very well lose the war and be overrun by the Germans. Would it be worth that indignity to know that I have let my countrymen down because I was afraid to go on? No, comrades, it is of vital importance that I make it to the United States. We won't let the Germans have the satisfaction of knowing that Rondonesleska succeeded, especially since he is dead. I will go on to the United States as planned."

"But sir, it could be very dangerous if you go on. If you go to the United States, the Japanese will treat you like an enemy agent if you are captured there. Remember that they had signed the Tripartite treaty with Germany."

"It is much too important that I make it to get the lend-lease aid, even if it means putting my own life in danger. We will go on to Alaska. After all, it is an order from my superiors in Moscow."

The Soviet official straightened up in a rigid stance. "Yes, sir, we will make immediate preparations for you and your family to reach Alaska safely."

Alexander had just joined his father. "We're not going to San Francisco?" His eyes narrowed in his displeasure of what he had just overheard.

Boris gently shook his head as he laid his hand on Alexander's shoulder. "No, we are not."

"But where is this Alaska? Will it be just like how you described San Francisco?"

"Not by a long shot. It is colder there than it is here!"

Alexander frowned. "Just what I didn't want to hear."

Boris was curious about the potential of the United States. He looked at the stiffly standing official and asked, "Were the Americans able to beat off the attack of the Japanese in Hawaii? What damage was inflicted on the United States Naval Forces?"

The official looked glum as he relayed the information that he had just received. "The information we have received so far is sketchy and incomplete, but our early reports are saying that most of the capital military vessels stationed at Pearl Harbor have either been sunk or severely damaged. The Americans were taken completely by surprise. According to radio reports, the Japanese ambassador did not break off negotiations until after the attack had commenced. It is almost certain that the Japanese have the upper hand now. It is suspected by many in the high command that the Japanese will be invading the Philippines and the Hawaiian Islands very soon." The official lifted his chin and stood firm. "In any case, the only alternative for you to reach the United States is through Alaska. It is highly unlikely that the Japanese will have any kind of force near the Chukchi Peninsula. Therefore, you are to proceed there as soon as you reach Vladivostok."

Boris shook his head slowly and muttered under his breath. "I was hoping that I would be going to a country where there would be no war. It was inevitable. The Americans are in everybody's way. They were doomed to get involved in this war."

All of this did not go unnoticed by the others who were standing by. There were serious implications that could be perceived. A nearby Russian soldier glanced uneasily into the air as new snowflakes drifted down into his face. Grimacing, he muttered, "It is now truly a world war."

CHAPTER 6

One off duty American G.I. had the unfortunate timing to be walking by Boris, who was coming out of his Quonset hut quarters. With his appointed rank as a lend-lease official, Boris Baranoff was accustomed to giving orders. It didn't matter to him if he was relaying instructions to Russian or American soldiers. What had always been the basis of the most importance were the badly needed weapons that were headed to the Soviet Union to defeat the Germans. Boris, in his quest, let little of any obstacle stand in his way to accomplish this goal.

Trying to quicken the work of loading the one lone ship in the harbor, Boris grumbled at the perceived slowness of the American soldiers as he related orders to them. He spoke to them in broken English and formed the speculation that they were deliberately trying to misunderstand him. In his opinion, American service men were far from perfect.

The Americans were far too independent in their thinking and Boris felt he was making little headway in convincing them to help the Soviet war machine.

Boris made this assumption after dealing with the U.S. soldiers for the last five months in the cold, harsh environment of the Aleutians. His opinion had not changed about the lazy capitalists, even though they were trying their best to accommodate him.

Boris still had to deal with his long-held prejudice of Americans and his patience was wearing thin. He was anxious to go home to a warm communist reception and take the last load of lend-lease supplies back to Russia.

His son, Alexander, was just as anxious to leave. His dissatisfaction was not because of the Americans, but it involved the continued boredom of the lonely and cold military base.

Alexander only could wish for someone his age that he could talk to so the days would go faster. The young teenager spent countless hours in restless thought and he wasted the majority of his time wandering up and down the rocky beach of the inlet.

Not everyone in his family seemed unhappy. Alexander noticed how cheerful his mother seemed to be just before he decided to go up a nearby mountain that day.

Alexander remembered the happier days in Leningrad as his mother began singing a Russian lullaby.

The words of her song even now frolicked in his mind.

> *May there always be sunshine.*
> *May there always be blue skies.*
> *May there always be Daddy.*
> *May there always be you.*

Even in the safety of Alaska, Alexander's mother seemed to search for some reason to be content, even putting in her own mind that she was glad to be away from the war-torn cities of her homeland.

Although there was no immediate danger here, Alexander had noticed that there was a hint of sadness in her voice as well.

Hoping to liven the spirits of his mother, Alexander walked up behind her as she worked at the stove. "Mama, do you ever miss the homeland?" Alexander asked softly.

Sonja Baranoff used her hand holding the wooden spoon to wipe her brow. Alexander couldn't tell if it was fatigue or just remembrance. With a definite shade of sadness upon her furrowed brow and in her gentle wispy voice, she responded, "I miss my friends. I miss the comfort of being able to talk to anyone that can understand me. The people here are nice, but they are all strangers." She gazed out the window with a faraway look. "Russia, my Russia. Sometimes I have the feeling I will never see her again. I remember the laughter and the sorrow, but she was the land I loved. And the people—oh the fun I had with the women back in Leningrad. The cooking times, the hundreds of quilts we sewed together. I could tell them some things I could never share with your father. Now I will never ever see some of them ever again." Sonja's eyes went downcast and Alexander heard her sniff. "And now I am in a strange land, a land that holds no memories for me. I want to go home to a land of peace and happiness. I only hope I can do it in my lifetime."

Alexander smiled optimistically. "We will, Mama. We will."

Sonja liked the encouragement and optimism that her son held. He was always a source of support for her. "I know that I am happy with you and Papa. As long as we are together, I can survive anywhere."

Some soldiers walked by the hut. It gave Alexander some optimism. With all the military activity in the area, Alexander had the strong belief that the war would remain far away from where he was now dwelling. Through his discussions with some of the army personnel, Alexander found out that everyone on the island believed that the Japanese would strike elsewhere for their continuing victories in the Pacific. The vicinity of the Aleutians Islands was not all that far away from the country of Japan, but there was the all around belief at Unalaska that the Japanese would prefer to fight in a warmer climate. The oil that the Japanese needed for their war against the British and the Americans existed in Indonesia and the Philippines. There was no incentive for the Japanese military to attack Alaska, except to kill Americans.

Alexander felt a sudden twinge of pain in his heart. His thoughts drifted once again to his homeland that seemed so far away. He knew that the hurting sensation in his mind and in his heart stemmed from the remembrance of the terrible ordeal his countrymen were going through in Russia. Alexander was positive that many of his brave and noble comrades were dying right at that moment. The news from the Soviet Union was unbearable. There was little that was mentioned in it except the never-ceasing and unmerciful attacks from the forces of Hitler's Third Reich. Letters from home were filled with the sad news of a great number of relatives that had already died. The deaths were not just from the Germans, but massive starvation was also contributing to the death toll. With the encircling siege of the city, news from Leningrad had suddenly ceased to exist. Alexander could only assume that the Nazis were now the conquerors of his home.

The young Russian couldn't help but feel nothing but hatred for the dictator of Germany. Hitler and his invading German troops were in his land, laying waste his beloved homeland and killing his friends and loved ones. There was a deep fear as well of this man. Despite knowing the fact that Hitler was halfway around the world, Alexander knew full well that his forces could conceivably reach Alaska, especially since they were pushing eastward across the Soviet Union. If German troops invaded Alaska, Boris and all of his family would be shot as enemies of the state for trying to obtain lend-lease supplies from the Americans. With things going the way they were, the possibility of the brutal little man with the short square moustache could soon be the absolute master of the Soviet Union and Europe was mounting daily.

Panic suddenly gripped Alexander as he focused on the very real possibility that even here in Alaska, the Germans could soon threaten his world. If by some unearthly reason that German troops would conquer the Soviet Union, more than likely their next aspirations would be to attack the Americans in Alaska. The possibility was very real. After all, didn't a German agent ride with him almost all the way across Russia on the train? Alaska was so large and sparsely populated that the Germans with the help of the Japanese could easily attack any where along the Alaskan coastline and not be dislodged.

Alexander thought about the corruptible Americans and their boasting. Their "nothing can beat us!" mentality sounded too much like what the Russians had been saying before Hitler's leagues pushed so far into the Soviet homeland. The young Russian lad knew they were boasting to help their morale, but most of the men sent here were being punished and they had little to be proud about in their military status. Many had been ordered to the Aleutians for insubordination. "Lucky you," he would tell them. "In Russia you would have been shot or sent to the salt mines of Siberia."

Alexander thought a lot of his new American friends and felt somewhat sorry for them and their cocky bourgeois ideology. "The Americans are so confident that their precious mainland soil is impervious to attack. They have no right to feel that way." Alexander knew better. "Can they see what is happening to Russia? Didn't the Japanese destroy their fleet at Pearl Harbor? Couldn't the Japanese just show up again out of nowhere?" Alexander directed his eyes on the American sailors all around the island and puckered his mouth in disgust. "If they could only see what has happened in my country. My father says that the Soviet people are the strongest in the world, yet they are losing the war. If the Americans are weaker than us, they don't stand a chance against the combined forces of Germany and Japan."

Alexander's head echoed the warning of his father. "Don't get involved with these weak-minded capitalists. They will only teach you to become lazy and will fill your head with nonsense that will eventually destroy you."

Alexander thought once again about his American sailor friends. "They weren't lazy or fat. Did his father know what he was talking about? He had even heard his father whisper to his mother that his stereotyping of Americans may have been premature. Alexander remembered, though, that it was only six months earlier that the Americans were caught off guard just like the Russians. The Japanese were successful because the Americans assumed that no one would attack them. The result was the humiliating defeat at Pearl Harbor in Hawaii. The lowly Japanese naval forces had beaten the Americans. "So what if it was a sneak attack."

That was no excuse. The Americans had been unprepared and that, in Alexander's frame of mind, was a sign of weakness in itself. It seemed now that the Americans were retreating on every battlefront against an enemy who was considered to be poor fighters. Alexander made up his mind there and then that the Americans were just as vulnerable as the Russians, perhaps even more so. There had even been an unconfirmed report that a Japanese submarine had shelled and landed troops in Oregon, one of the northwestern states, without so much as a tiny bit of opposition to the invasion. There were constant rumors on the base about when the Japanese would invade Dutch Harbor.

Alexander was appalled at how the Americans almost regarded the impending danger as a game. "Wait until they kill your closest friends. You will take this war a little more seriously," he scorned some of the American sailors who had become friends with him.

"I know what has happened in Russia and why you seem so bitter," responded a sailor. "But let me tell you this, we have no love for the Axis powers either. We're just as frightened as you are and we know that if the Japanese attack, we will probably lose friends just like you did. I lost three good buddies and a brother at Pearl Harbor. You must believe me when I say this is no game to me. I want to avenge my country for my brother's sake and for all the others that died on December 7th."

Alexander believed what he was hearing and set off on his own to think about all the possibilities that a war would bring to the world at that moment.

Alexander was beginning to feel a little impatient. He sniffed the air as he went by the little Quonset hut where he and his parents were staying. He smelled something wonderful. His mother had started cooking baklava. For a brief moment, Alexander imagined a better time at his home in Russia. "Mother is probably humming that song right now as she cooks." Alexander smiled at the thought.

His mind soon shifted back to the activities of the base. Foreign voices interrupted his thinking. The base was too noisy. Alexander spied the mountain that he had longed to climb ever since he had arrived at Dutch Harbor. Even though he was told not to leave the base, Alexander felt that it was time to be away from the military base by himself. The young man started up the moderate slope of Mount Ballyhoo, but not before he had a chance to talk to his mother.

Sonja looked out the window to the bustling horde of army men and noticed that some of them were responding to rays of the sun that had just broken through the clouds. "Ah, the sun is beginning to shine. Why don't you go out and enjoyed the fresh air for a while?"

Alexander eagerly put on his grayish green coat and fur-lined hat. He shifted his eyes to a peak that overlooked the harbor. "I think I will explore that mountain today—the one the American sailors called Mount Ballyhoo."

Sonja nodded. "Have fun. Remember to keep your parka on, for the winds seem to be especially fierce around here, even more so than what we went though in Siberia. Oh, and one more thing, be sure you come back before supper."

Alexander waved and slipped out the door. He would enjoy her meal later on. Climbing the mountain would surely increase his appetite.

In no time at all, Alexander was standing on the bleak rocky knoll overlooking the Aleutian American base of Dutch Harbor.

Alexander recovered from reminiscing as a new burst of wind pounded his face. He turned and looked up to the summit of Ballyhoo. He longed to go higher and proceeded up the hill. Alexander felt the chill of the first barbs of wind as he climbed the knoll that overlooked the U.S. army base of Dutch Harbor in Unalaska, one of the major islands of the Aleutian chain jutting southwest from Alaska. Despite the cold strong winds, spring had come to the Arctic island and the small sprigs of juniper bushes were already turning green.

The young Russian leaned into the gusts of wind and fought to maintain his balance. Along with the callous winds, came the rugged beauty of the landscape. The snow-covered emerald green peaks and the windswept ocean stretched out before him. The Aleutians' winds, called "williwaws" by the American soldiers, were strong and cold.

Alexander peered across the bay at the high pinnacles of rocks of the island. There was a sense of foreboding and disquieting uneasiness about this bleak island called Unalaska. The sharp winds from the northwest stung his face with cold bursts as he stood on the exposed slope. He felt somewhat helpless and lonely. However, along with the callous winds, was the rugged beauty of the landscape. The snow covered peaks and the windswept ocean stretched out before him.

Closer to Alexander's location, near the base of the mountain, was the army base where U.S. personnel went about their usual duties with one exception: some were performing a new duty by hauling lend-lease supplies into the one lone cargo ship. Down below him near the waterfront, there was a mire of activity around the dock near the *Northwestern*, the reputed derelict transport ship.

Local army commanders were hoping that the ship would appear to be out of commission from the air. Alexander stared silently from the mountain as a huge crane lifted the cargo nets full of crates into the hold of the ship. Information had leaked out that this supposedly empty supply ship that was to be used as crew quarters for some of the navel personnel. The fact of the matter was that this apparently derelict vessel was actually a supply ship, which was being loaded with lend-lease hidden reserves of weapons. The destination was to be kept a secret, but everyone on the island knew where these weapons were going, because of the three Russians on the island. The only possibility was the Soviet Union. The ship was under the disguise of temporary crew quarters just in case there was any air surveillance by the Japanese. The enemy troops were supposed to believe that the *Northwestern* was dead in the water. The navel personnel tried to persuade this Axis partner of the east that this farce was genuine by having certain crewmen bring in sleeping bags every night.

Not only was this trickery put into practice every night to fool the enemy in the air, but it was also used in case the Japanese had some scouts who had been landed on the island of Unalaska in secret.

Soldiers and dock workers milled around the base like busy ants amid the wooden buildings near the dock. The bay itself was involved with a flurry of activity, stemming with loading of the supposedly derelict *Northwestern*, with tons of wooden crates and war supplies, all which were bound for the Soviet Union.

From his vantage point, standing on the slope of the highest mountain, Mount Ballyhoo, Alexander could clearly see across the harbor down below him. The landscape of Unalaska presented Alexander with a magnificent view of green mountains whose pinnacles were laced with frosty glittering snow, but Alexander was not thinking about the scenery. There was a sense of foreboding and disquieting apprehension about the bleak island.

As it had been on the Trans-Siberian railroad, there was no one his age on this forlorn island outpost of Alaska that he could share similar ideas and talk to about his feelings. Life in Alaska, as it had been in Siberia, was quite dull and boring with only the constant barrage of U.S. army and navy personnel on hand to converse with, many of whom had no time for a Russian teenager. To Alexander, they were complete strangers.

The fact that made this seem worse was that this land wasn't even his country. Everything about this island was different and alien to him. His English was just good enough to hold a limited conversation with the Americans, but nothing beyond that, not that he had much to say to them anyway.

Despite all the new people and unique sights, Alexander was certain that he didn't want to stay here long. The last eight months of his life had been spent in the snow. He had enough of it riding on the train. He tried his best to adapt to the new situation. Overall the American military men were trying their best to be cordial to him.

Alexander had learned above everything else—the Aleutian Islands were a very inhospitable place to be if you were expecting good weather and good company. The soldiers hated it here and there were a few that took it out on the foreign dignitaries.

Alexander crossed his arms as he heard the distant approach of the wind again. The williwaws, swept in from the northwest coming in from the Bering Strait. This was the passageway that Virtus Bering sailed on between Alaska and Russia in the year of 1740.

Alexander thought about the ancient claim of the explorer of Alaska. He remembered the lessons of history from his native land. He had been taught by several soviet educators that the old ruler, the tsar, had made a major blunder in 1867 in selling Alaska to the

United States. The price was cheap, less than two cents per acre. The resources found later in Alaska were a major blow to the prestige of the Russian nation. There were other repercussions as well: another rival close by. "If only our country had kept Alaska instead of giving it to the Americans, we wouldn't have another antagonist with land so close to ours."

Alexander felt a little annoyed upon remembering the harsh history lesson he had recently been taught by his father. "How could we ever have made that mistake of practically giving them this land?" Alexander frowned and shook his head. The forces of nature brought him back to the present. Alexander felt the breeze on his face as the young man glimpsed towards the direction of his homeland. The Soviet Union was only a few hundred miles away, but knowing all of this only made the boy feel lonelier for his home.

A small wisp of smoke rose from the smokestack of the hut. He looked down below to see the Quonset hut where his mother was preparing one of his favorite dishes, Kartofelnyie Kotlety (potato pancakes). The despair in his mind was made worst by the fact that his mother, down below in the Quonset hut, was making one of his favorite dishes that was definitely a Russian original, another reminder of his distant home. Leningrad was virtually on the other side of the world now. Alexander shook his head in despondency. "I will never get used to America!"

Alexander shivered as he climbed a little higher up on the lichen covered tundra knoll that overlooked the U.S. army base of Dutch Harbor on the island of Unalaska. "Why do the Aleutians have to be so barren? Siberia was bad enough; now I have to deal with the cold winds of Alaska," Alexander wondered as he wrapped up tighter in his parka.

Another burst of wind hit Alexander in the face. Alexander leaned into the gusts and fought to maintain his balance. From his vantage point on Mount Ballyhoo, the young Russian could see clear across the harbor.

Men milled around the base like busy ants amid the wooden buildings and dock buildings.

Alexander peered at the ocean in the distance. The sound of the waves echoed in his ears. It was quite peaceful here even though the United States was at war. Their war was far away in the South Pacific. There were no similarities to what was occurring here and what was taking place in Russia, except for the constant cold breezes.

Another problem faced by the Russians was the cold hard fact that in sailing the supplies back to the Soviet Union, they would have to travel near America's enemy in the Pacific, Japan. This was a good situation for the Soviets for the time being because supplies could still reach Vladivostok without Japanese interference. The Soviet Union, unlike the Americans, wanted to defeat Hitler first before concentrating on the Japanese.

All this activity was fascinating to Alexander. At fourteen years of age, the young man had an insatiable curiosity about such events, especially since there was very little else to do on this bleak barren shoal off the coast of the Island of Unalaska. In his eagerness to explore this strange new land, Alexander went beyond the usual safety procedures. He was warned many times by the base commanders and his own father not to wander too far from the military outpost. Rumors spread rapidly every day that the Japanese were nearby. Alexander was told to stay close by just in case the Japanese decided to invade Dutch Harbor. The memory of that morning was fresh in his mind. Hunger pangs seeped into Alexander's stomach and he was resolved to head back down the mountain. He wanted to look around one last time. The memory faded and Alexander gazed once more at the activity below him. He had heard some rumors that he would be going home to Russia with his parents soon on the *Northwestern*. His last glimpse of America might be right at that moment.

Alexander tucked his hands into his coat pockets and rotated his eyes and surveyed the barren landscape of the rocky island he was now occupying. The mountains nearby cast a certain chill and loneliness with their mantle of granite and snowy slopes that appeared bleak to Alexander. There was an air of beauty about these massive giants as they lay across the bay from him. Unalaska in a way, reminded the young man of his home back in Leningrad. The similarities mainly had to do with the coldness. There was harshness about the land that he had felt in Leningrad. There was still snow on the mountains here and he was already accustomed to the harsh winters of Leningrad.

However, there was very little else, except for the coldness that could remind him of home. Leningrad was marshy and flat. Unalaska was mountainous and rocky. More importantly, the Nazis were ravaging his homeland. There were no murdering Germans here. The war in Russia was distant.

The young boy bundled his parka close to him and he pushed his head deeper inside his fur-lined hood. He still felt the retreating winds of the last williwaws coming out of the north. He still wondered if the war would soon be with him on Unalaska. Maybe it was just a feeling, but Alexander was already accustomed to death and war. The idea in his mind was strong. The war would follow him here. He was positive that it would happen sooner than expected.

Suddenly, Alexander had a nagging uneasy tenseness in his brain. It put a strangle hold on his feelings and told him that something awful was about to happen. Alexander turned his ears away from the wind in trying to figure out what had caused his strange premonition of danger. All he could hear was the pounding of the surf down below him. It was strangely quiet, even with the winds that had suddenly died down. He looked down from the slope of the mountain, Mount Ballyhoo, where he had been watching the whole U.S. military contingent. They still acted like they would be safe from the whole world. "The fools," he thought. "When will they get it straight in their minds that a world war is going on?" Alexander grimaced as he began to wander down, disgusted at their nonchalant attitude.

The Russian boy was well on his way when he suddenly stopped in his tracks halfway down the side of the hill. He strained to listen through the winds and swore he could hear some type of continuous plane engine buzzing in the distance. The vibration of the plane engine was loud enough now that Alexander was positive that it was coming from the air behind him on the other side of the mountain. He strained to see where the sound was headed but the clouds were too thick to see through except right over the island. There was one huge blue hole lingering over Dutch Harbor. If these were indeed enemy bombers, they would see what they were aiming for any second. Alexander's pace quickened to get down the slope. The young Russian boy had been at Dutch Harbor long enough to know the sounds of the American P-40s and the reverberation did not belong to that type of plane. The planes were definitely not American.

The realization of complete anxiety for the boy was suddenly very real. Alexander realized at that moment that he was listening to enemy bombers, but which country was sending these vessels of death.

The roar of the engines overhead grew louder. Alexander looked down at the people on the base. They were beginning to react to the sound of the planes. Alexander had just barely turned back to see what was causing the noise, when suddenly the vision of two bright solid red circles on the wings of three airplanes flashed in his eyes. It seemed as if the planes had just lunged out of the clouds right at Alexander.

Alexander instinctively ducked as the olive and gray colored-planes passed within a hundred feet of where he was standing. He could clearly see the pilots in their cockpits and they could see him. One man in the second plane pointed to Alexander as if to get the other flyers to strafe him. The young boy saw the other pilot shaking his head. They had more important targets. The planes headed down toward the army base. The sky was suddenly filled with smoke and flame.

Alexander crouched behind a huge boulder. He could hardly believe what was going on in front of him, but he had no doubts now about the nationality of the attacking war birds. He could clearly see the emblazing red circles on the wing tips—the attacking planes were Japanese Zeroes.

CHAPTER 7

All at once it appeared that the entire island of Unalaska as if it was erupting in front of the young Russian boy. The ominous roar of several planes filled the air, followed by numerous blasts of flak. The landscape below in the compound was immediately dominated by the sudden burst of continuous gunfire and quick successions of explosions.

Alexander felt the cold chill of fear go down his spine as he once again proceeded down the hill to seek protection in one of the bomb shelters. Amid the confusion of smoke and fire the young man was hoping that the Japanese wouldn't concern themselves with him. Out on the exposed slope, he was an easy target.

The scene below Alexander was one of complete chaos. Ground personnel tried to fight back the best they could with small arms fire and machine guns. Men were blindly trying to run through the smoke and the explosions amid the newly formed rubble. More bombs lunged out of the sky. As each black explosive device hit the surface of the earth, an eruption of red and orange flame rocked the landscape. Every bomb detonated and had found its victim with violent projectiles of shrapnel.

Alexander opened his mouth in astonishment as two more gray single engines planes lunged right above him as if they had just popped out of the nearby clouds. The bright red solid circles on the wings of the Zeroes made Alexander momentarily wonder why the Japanese had bother to keep the rest of the plane gray. If the reason was for camouflage purposes, they were an absolute atrocity.

The young man's mind quickly raced back to the purpose of the deadly raid. He quickly tried to remember where he had last seen his parents.

As explosions began to rock the air, Alexander realized that the

Japanese pilots presently were not concerned about a youthful Russian civilian who was hiding. They were looking for live military targets.

The young Russian boy fearfully observed the unfolding drama, transfixed and enthralled as the war planes descended down towards their prey near the bay. Alexander could see the navy men near the *Northwestern* were just now beginning to react to the air raid, trying to run helter-skelter away from the ship.

Alexander thought briefly about the mission of the ship and knew that the ship would probably be sunk soon. He quickly considered other options for going home, but it was irrelevant now. His attention was diverted back quickly to the succession of bombs that tumbled down from the planes, indiscriminately falling on military and innocent targets.

The young Russian teenager watched in horror as bombs started plummeting to the ground in rapid succession near the Quonset hut where his family had been staying. He gasped in disbelief for he knew his mother was still inside the Quonset hut, probably huddled in a corner of the building.

The young man suddenly stopped midway down the sandy hillside to keep himself from falling forward. Alexander ducked instinctively as a bomb dislodged and exploded near him on the hill.

The planes continued to let loose a series of bombs on the military complex. One bomb, as if guided by a wire, fell directly towards the little half-circle tin building where his family had been staying. The wisps of white vapors from the smokestack indicated that his mother had been preparing the morning meal. Alexander felt a sickening sensation go through his stomach as he watched the bomb go right through the roof near the smokestack. The young man pulled in his head into his shoulders as a reaction to the inevitable explosion.

For a brief second, it appeared as if the bomb was not going to detonate. "Nothing happened. It's a dud," he fervently hoped.

Suddenly a bright red and orange flash came from out of the Quonset hut with a thunderous blast. The next thing that Alexander could see was black smoke billowing out of an empty twisted steel frame.

The young Russian was wishing among all hope that this was all just a terrible nightmare. His guts tightened within his wretched teenage frame. He desperately wanted to wake up from this terrible ordeal of death and destruction.

Alexander stood there motionless at a peculiar angle on the hillside with one foot lower than the other to prevent himself from sliding down on the loose sand and rock. The scene was too much to comprehend and bear. Alexander fought hard to accept the reality, but yet it was true. He stood there shaking all over looking down on the military post. The scene was full of death and carnage and he looked on it in disbelief and shock. Then the realization of the truth hit him hard. His mother was dead. He began to feel his body fill with sorrowful anger at the thought of the senseless killing that had just taken place.

There was little time to think about what had just happened. The Japanese planes were beginning to find other targets. Many of the military individuals had not yet found adequate cover and the Zeroes were quick to find them. Planes came in from every direction and they maneuvered into position where their deadly machines would try to strafe everyone who was running for a foxhole or bomb shelter.

Each explosion from the deadly bombs changed the surrounding island into a labyrinth of shell holes where military buildings once stood. Reaction to the Zeroes was quick, but there was little the anti-aircraft defenses could do against the murderous planes. The Japanese planes were too fast. The huge guns of the base tried to respond to the fast moving Zeroes, but they could not pivot fast enough to keep the planes in their sights. Nevertheless, they continued firing in fanatic desperation as the shore gunners tried to protect the lives of everyone on the island.

Alexander regained some sense of his surroundings and jumped into a freshly made bomb crater on the side of Mount Ballyhoo. He covered his ears in an attempt to drown out the tremendous explosions of the bombs as well as the resounding cracking bursts coming from the shore batteries. Alexander peered out of the hole and saw his father running along the wooden dock with two American sailors. They had just come out of the ship *Northwestern* and were trying to reach the safety of the bomb shelters near the Siems-Drake warehouse.

Boris tripped over a knothole in the dock and dropped his clipboard with the list of medical and military supplies that were suppose to help the Soviet Union. Without those valuable papers, Russian supplies could be minuscule and untraceable. Boris tried to retrieve the valuable document and was slow to get up. The two sailors helped him to his feet and they began running again.

Alexander knew by the direction the three men were running that they were trying to reach the end of the dock where it would be possible to climb down and hide in a dugout shelter.

One plane swooped down quickly and the pilot fixed his sights on the helpless men running on the dock. There was no chance now that they would reach the bomb shelter. The small delay in reaching for the clipboard made death a certainty.

Alexander's eyes went upwards from behind his father who was now running for his very existence. "If he could only reach the ladder, he'll be safe."

Alexander envisioned in his mind that hope was quickly fading. "Run, Father, Run!" From the corner of his eye, the young Russian spotted the Zero beginning to make a strafing run right for his father.

Alexander could see clearly what the attacking plane was intending to do. The gray and green plane was coming in quite low and converging towards the dock area where Boris was sprinting for the ladder.

Boris, running for all he was worth, was only fifty feet from the ladder. Tracers blazed from the Zero's machine guns, splintering wood in a straight line aimed right at the men on the dock.

Alexander heard himself utter. "Only a few more feet, you can make it!" His cries of hope were a useless gesture.

The Zero picked up speed and its guns were blazing, seeking to kill the quarry on the ground. For what seemed to be an enternity, Alexander watched as the strafing bullets kicked up wood shavings and splinters in a track from the sea towards his father and the two sailors. Alexander cupped his hands around his mouth in an attempt to yell at the men to dive in the water. The words didn't even have time to leave his lips. Death had arrived.

One sailor caught three of the tracer bullets in his back as he buckled to his knees. He attempted in a death grip to grab for his back with one hand. He crumpled to the wooden deck. The second sailor spun like a top as a slug caught him in the side. The impact of more bullets twisted him as he splashed into the water.

Boris looked behind him to see what had happened to his body-guards. Sensing increasing panic, he failed to grab the top rung of the ladder on the first try.

Boris was never allowed to make a second attempt. On his second try, tracers found him. The large Russian went down to his knees covering two holes in his chest. In great pain he used all his remaining strength and slowly turned his head to look up to the mountain where he had last seen his son. "The Zeroes, where are they?" He struggled to see through the smoky haze. The horrible carnage of the dead and dying was all around him. The acrid smell of black gunpowder was thick and heavy and it stung the inside of his nose.

"Alexander? Sonja? Are they all right?" In great pain, Boris could see that the Japanese planes were retreating.

Squinting to look up through the last of the evaporating smoke and dust, Boris could see that his son was still on the side of Mount Ballyhoo, safe and unharmed

With a weak smile of reassuring relief, Boris slowly took on a prostrate position, his hand nearly touching the top rung of the ladder that would have led him to safety. He crumpled to the wooden beams of the dock. With a final gasp, his eyes fluttered closed forever.

Alexander looked up in absolute fury at the planes that were retiring back to their carriers, but knew he was helpless to do anything about it. Blinded by rage, Alexander picked up a rock, intending to hurl it at the retreating planes. The boy slowly dropped his head in shame. He slammed the rock down to the ground in vehement fervor.

Alexander's immediate reaction was one of indignation. "Why did we ever come to this…this Alaska?" There was a feeling of guilt because he was the only one left alive in his family. "Why hadn't the Japanese killed me as well?" Alexander quickly dismissed this notion out of his head. His father had told him once or twice that suicide was only for cowards.

Regaining a little bit of his composure, Alexander made his way down the mountainside and slowly made his way to where his father was lying dead on his side. Four bullet holes bled profusely from his back.

Shuffling through the mass of men who were climbing out of bomb craters and bomb shelters, the boy stumbled as if he were in a daze. The attack of the Japanese had lasted only a few minutes, but the effect of the raid was devastating. At least twenty men were lying dead in the compound.

Alexander peered into the sky, his eyes transfixed on a single cloud. The young Russian tried to focus his thoughts on being brave to keep the tears from coming out, but it was no use. The attempt was in vain. Pride was now a useless gesture. His only thoughts were on his parents and how they had died. The whole situation seemed surreal to him. Gritting his teeth, Alexander squinted at the bloody scene below him near the dock. Every step he took felt heavy as he meandered around the dead and the dying. His only gaze was set straight ahead and there was hardly any vision. All he could see was a huge blurry picture for his eyes were blotted with gigantic tears.

Alexander tried to reach his father on the dock through the massive devastation. Two American sailors tried to hold him back. "Alexander, stay here with us. It's no use. They're gone," one tried to comfort him.

The young Russian held his ground for a moment. The tears came out quickly as reality finally hit him. The sailors relaxed their grip. Slowly the young Russian reached the place where his father was lying. The young man crumpled to his knees and let out a cry of anguish. His head fell upon his father's lifeless body.

Sailors continued to run around the young man, checking the

dead and wounded. Some were hesitant to move around and many kept scanning the skies to make sure the marauding Japanese planes didn't return. Three of the sailors stopped in their tracks as they discovered that one of the bodies was that of the large Russian consulate and mediator for the lend-lease material. Two of the sailors looked at Alexander, who barely noticed their presence. His hands were clenched and drawn up to his mouth.

In his grief, Alexander tried to reason in his mind why the lend-lease program to obtain weapons for his country was so important that it cost the lives of both his parents. "We should have never come to Alaska! We were better off in the Soviet Union." Alexander angrily declared to the men watching him, "This war with the Japanese was none of our concern. Why? Why did I have to come here? Just to see my parents get killed?" Alexander broke down and yielded to his grief and bowed his body forward, trying to bury his face into the earth. With the tears streaming down his face, he asked, "What will I do now?"

The sailors bent their heads in sorrow. They had lost friends in the attack, but it was plain to see that Alexander had lost his family. The three service men walked off to tend to the wounded that were still moving. Alexander would be left alone for the time being with his pain and sorrow.

More men came running from the bomb shelters to assess the damage to the base. The commanding officer noticed the lifeless body of Alexander's father, with the young boy crying over him.

Shaking his head in concern, Lieutenant Roy Evans summoned two sailors to his side. Indicating with a motion of his hand, Evans whispered to the blue jackets, "Make sure you detain him and make him understand that he must stay near the base. He will want to go home now and I am certain that there is no way to return him to the Soviet Union at this time. The Japs are sure to be watching for any attempt to go west. In fact, they may have already positioned submarines between Alaska and Russia. My bet is that they will try to take the western Aleutians now. That will make it impossible for Alexander to go home. Our young friend there will have to stick around for a while." Lieutenant Evans looked up and spotted the burning ship that was supposed to take the Russians back home. Half of the *Northwestern* was in flames. Frowning, Evans stared at the obliterated vessel. "We were going to send him home in that ship. There's no chance of that now."

The young officer grimaced at the devastating destruction in the compound. All around him, the dead and the wounded were littered on the ground. His hand covered his face to hide the hate and the fear. "God, I hate this war."

The flames from the obliterated ship and nearby storehouses began to subside as men began to evacuate the shelters where they had hid from the Japanese tracers and bombs. There were new duties to perform and fresh thoughts were put into motion as the necessity of adapting to the war became apparent.

Evans sent one man to report the situation to the base commander, Captain William Updegraff. Advising him of the situation, Second class torpedo man Christopher Troy Phillips stood by as Commander Updegraff telephoned Brigadier General William O. Butler of the strategic air command of the southwest Alaskan area.

"General, our situation here is critical and we have at least twenty casualties. We have also lost the Soviet overseer for the lend-lease program. We may have lost the *Northwestern* as well. She has taken on some damage. Most of the supplies that were scheduled for Vladivostok have been destroyed in the Siems-Drake warehouse. There is the possibility that we can expect another attack fairly soon. The Japanese must have at least one aircraft carrier nearby."

"Were the Russians in the bomb shelter during the raid?"

"No sir, they were not."

"What in the world were the Russians doing outside during a raid?" the general asked gruffly.

The captain cleared his throat nervously. "Mr. Baranoff was checking his list of supplies on the *Northwestern* when the raid began. He didn't have much of a chance to reach the bomb shelter. His wife, Sonja, was in the Quonset hut and it took a direct hit."

The general spoke up. "Did anyone survive of the Russian delegation?"

Captain Updegraff cleared his throat. "Both Boris and his wife

Sonja were killed, but their son is still alive. He was away from the encampment when the Japanese Zeroes hit the island."

The general curled his lips. "Drat it all. Nincompoops are running this man's army." He blurted out louder. "So only young Baranoff lived?"

"Yes sir!"

"What is the young man's name, Captain?"

"I believe it is Alexander, sir! Spelled A-L-E-X-A-N-D-E-R."

"Captain, our relations with the Soviets have been delicate to say the least. There is still the question if they might join the radicals in Japan to fight us. We must not give them an excuse. This boy must be kept safe at all costs. In fact, I want him taken off that base. Find a place for him on the mainland."

The general was handed some documents and could sense that the captain was ready to hang up the phone. "And I mean a place where the Germans and Japs will never find him. I don't want to be responsible for starting a war with the Russians. I have enough problems trying to explain how his parents were killed. Keeping this boy alive will help cement a closer tie with Stalin and we need the Russian people to keep the Germans off our back. Is everything clear? "

"Yes sir!"

"We cannot jeopardize future operations with the Russians. We need to keep Alexander Baranoff alive and out of Japanese hands. Find a place for him immediately. The information he carries in his head about his father's orders would be too valuable to the Axis powers."

"I understand completely, sir. Alexander will be put on the first available Catalina. I have a friend on the mainland near Soldotna. Maybe he will be able to take Alexander in for a little while."

"Very well, carry on."

The captain hung up the phone and turned to go out to an awaiting jeep. Captain Updegraff boarded the vehicle and informed the driver, "Take off. I have some hard decisions to make."

Captain Updegraff raised his finger as another thought came to him. "Were there any other documents or papers with Mr. Baranoff that need to be destroyed or taken out of here?"

"No sir! I don't believe so."

The captain was miffed. "Are there or are there not?"

The sailor stiffened. "No sir, there are none. Just the boy." He couldn't believe that the captain would compare documents to a human being.

"Well, it has been decided. Here is what you need to do once we get back to the dock area." They took off in the jeep.

Once back near the dock, Captain Updegraff commanded the sailor to find Alexander and put him on a Catalina Flying boat. It was expected that the plane would be crowded. There would be some extra passengers because some of the wounded had to be transported to better facilities.

Arriving at his office, Updegraff picked up the phone and called Major Thomas Brendan Hunt, a friend in the town of Soldotna on the Kenai Peninsula. He was hoping to make arrangements with the major who lived in Soldotna on the Kenai Peninsula.

"Brendan? Hi. I have a little favor to ask of you."

"I can imagine." the voice retorted at the other end. "So what is it?"

"I have a boy here that just lost his parents. Could you keep him there with you for just a little while?"

"How long is a little while?"

"Until we figure out how to get him back to the Soviet Union. Hopefully not too long."

"The Soviet Union, do you mean he's a Russian?"

"Yes, he is. I hope that's not a big problem for you."

Major Hunt sighed. "No, bring him here. We'll try to accommodate him."

"It's just that I need to place him in a safe place. He has information that the Japs could use if they got a hold of him. Can you take him off my hands until the area between Alaska and Russia is cleared?"

"I said okay, but just for a little while. I have a family to think about."

"Thanks, Brendan. I owe you one. We'll fly him up there as soon as possible. He should be at the Kenai docks in three, maybe four hours." Hanging up the phone, Updegraff sent an officer to the Catalina to make sure that the order would be carried out to put the young Russian on board the seaplane.

The Catalina pilot was unsure about sticking around. "But sir, what if the Japs return while I am still tied up to the dock?"

"You have your orders. Wait until we know for sure that the boy is going to Soldotna."

"Yes sir." The pilot glared outside at his potential passenger. *Dumb kid, he is going to get us all killed.*

After a brief command, the two sailors that were standing close by to Alexander moved in towards the boy. Alexander was unaware of their presence and continued to lament for his father. Alexander sniffed and his tears began to subside. Boris had once told him that crying was only for the weak. Alexander felt anything but strong. In his confused and disoriented state, Alexander failed to see the two sailors coming up behind him.

"It's time to go, son."

CHAPTER 8

In the wake of all the death and destruction that surrounded him, Alexander failed to see the two seamen coming for him. The husky men frantically scanned the skies and they made their way towards the Russian youngster.

Caught up in a daze because of his parents' death, Alexander could hardly feel himself being pulled up by his feet by the two men who had been ordered to put him on the PBY.

At first, the young Russian believed that the men were there to comfort him as they handled him gently at first. Alexander focused on the circumstances and soon discovered that he was being dragged to the dock area where a Flying PBY was revving up and waiting for him. The two sailors were holding him tight.

When Alexander finally realized the magnitude of the situation, he began pulling away from his would-be rescuers. "Where are you taking me?" he asked in broken English.

"To a place where you will be safe from the Japanese when they land here," one of the sailors lashed back just as roughly. "Now cooperate with us. We need you to get on board the plane." The sailor had no time to be nice in this type of situation and the life of the young Russian depended on how fast the sailor could move his unwilling passenger.

"I cannot let you take me away without a proper burial for my father and my mother. You must let me stay!" Alexander temporarily broke away from the two men. He grabbed a nearby steel post and dug in with his heels.

As the men advanced, Alexander let go of the post and ran unwillingly to the dock. He was trapped.

The sailors chased him down. One of the men tried to grab the youngster by the arm. He was frustrated by the antics of the teenager. Angrily he shouted, "You can't stay here. The Japs won't be asking what country you are from when they get here. They'll be shooting anything that moves and that includes impertinent Russian teenagers. Now come back here!"

The larger sailor caught the young Russian by the scuff of the neck to make his point clear. Alexander struggled briefly and decided not to resist any longer.

"So where am I going?"

"To the mainland of Alaska if we can get you there in one piece!" The sailor was filled with pessimism. Alexander couldn't help but notice that in his brief encounter with this particular sailor, how this man was always being sarcastic. "Hopefully, the Japs won't come back for a while or be bold enough to patrol the waters north of here. They'll have us for shark bait if they spot our Catalina with one of their planes."

The salty air of the ocean breeze rippled towards the trio, leaving no indication of the conflict that had just taken place. It had a small calming effect on the individuals.

Alexander relaxed and sadly looked back at the obliterated Quonset hut that had been his temporary home and where his mother had died. The smoldering debris crackled with the last flickering flames around the damaged skeleton half-circle frame that had once been a Quonset hut.

The air was heavy with the scent of acidic gunpowder smoke and sickening death. Sailors were already removing the bodies of both his parents. What remained of his mother was covered by a black tarp and it only required one man to carry it. The sight was more than Alexander could endure. He buried his face into the cusp of his arm.

Alexander remembered the warmth of his mother in contrast to the rough exterior of his father. They had been quite different from each other, but their love was strong. "I had to hand it to mother for putting up with me," but he didn't mind her putting him in line. "I don't think I want to go on!" The young man struggled enough to make the escorting sailors stop in their tracks. Alexander's wish was to see his mother once more. He wasn't even allowed a chance to say goodbye to her. The young man felt helpless and angry that she would have to die in a foreign land—a place many in his nation considered unfriendly. His only consolation was the fact that she had died quickly.

The sailors continued to escort the young Russian over the very same dock where his father had been killed by the Zero's bullets. With a sullen indignation of wanting to strike at an enemy that is nowhere to be seen, Alexander decided to take out his anger on the people dragging him away from the area. His mind couldn't help but think of what it was like for his parents to be killed from a plane while they were walking on the ground unprotected. Alexander could feel the hatred mounting within his body for the Japanese. He had heard many stories from the Americans about the alleged atrocities committed by the Imperial troops. Alexander was ready to believe them. His hate for the Japanese was stronger even now than his hate for the Nazis.

The reeking vapors of burning gunpowder and the putrid salty brine combined to produce a nauseating stench. The smell would not last long. The williwaws kicked up once more, blowing away the deadly scent and causing white caps to form on the waters of the bay. The water of Dutch Harbor became rough and choppy.

An old PBY seaplane tied up near by on the dock began bobbing up and down like a cork in a barrel of water. Alexander felt the tears streaming down his face once again. Everything was so unreal and strange to him. His head pounded in frustration. The whole gruesome scenario reminded him of the terror he had felt in Leningrad. At that moment, with everything feeling alien to him, Alexander couldn't help but believe that life was meaningless. There was a real fear of what his future would be like too. He still wasn't completely sure where these cold-hearted Americans were taking him. They told him Alaska, but they refused to confide in Alexander where he would be headed in that territory. They had refused to tell him anything claiming that if the Japanese were able to shoot the plane down and capture him, he could reveal the destination of most of the American planes.

Alexander finally realized that he would be safer in the wide wilderness of the Alaskan territory than where he was standing now, or if he tried to reach his homeland. Alexander could only hope that his stay in America would not be that long. "How long will it be before they will allow me to go home?"

He guessed correctly that it wouldn't be anytime soon since he was headed to the mainland of Alaska. The reverberation of an airplane engine made him look up. A waiting royal blue Catalina seaplane was floating near the bullet-riddled dock nearby. The PBY's engines had already been prepared for takeoff as Alexander was forced into it. The floating plane was a strange sight with the single wing over the top of the body that looked liked a big blue banana with a blue star painted inside a white circle on the side of it. Alexander was jammed in the passenger compartment with four wounded sailors and six non-combatants, some of who had worked with his father on the lend-lease arrangements. The compartment was cramped and there was very little room to move around. Everyone strong enough to stand up had to cock their head sideways because of the curved ceiling. There was a mixture of salt water and aviation fuel vapors in the air. There was still a trace of sulfur and gunpowder from the raid. Everyone in the plane's passenger compartment dropped his or her heads in private sorrow and compassion as Alexander entered the plane. They knew the young man was facing a hard time.

Two sailors were lying next to the bulkhead of the fuselage and another civilian worker was sitting next to the young Russian. This man was nervous. He knew very well that the Japanese might still have some pilots in the air. Their Zeroes could easily out maneuver the old Catalina. Death was still in the air, somewhere.

From his vantage point, Alexander could see up into the cockpit where two naval officers were controlling the plane. They almost seemed oblivious to their passengers.

The seaplane was quickly released from its moorings on the pier and the pilot began to rev up the engines of the PBY to prepare it for the air. The engines roared so loud that people inside the plane almost had to shout to be heard.

The pilot began to operate and manipulate the plane away from the dock. Alexander peered through the small port window trying to get a final glimpse of the place where his parents had died. He sat back trying to forget the horrifying memory of their deaths. Soon the plane was in a position for takeoff. As the plane began to take up speed, Alexander bounced around like a rubber ball. He could feel and hear the waves pounding against the steel structure of the PBY. It was as if the water was trying to keep the plane from taking off.

The pilot shouted back to the passengers. "You better buckle in the best you can. We might have a rough time of it trying to get out of the water."

"What's the problem?" Alexander asked one of the nearby wounded sailors.

"Too much weight," the sailor came back with a muffled reply. "We may not get out of the water!"

"Hey, if there are too many people on board and you can't get this plane out of the water, go ahead and turn around. I'd be happy to stay put on Unalaska Island."

"You stay put just where you are. We'll get off this ocean if I have to pick up my feet a thousand times. We'll make it all right," shouted the pilot trying to be heard over the engines.

Alexander returned to his seat, but did not use the buckle. He saw no reason for safety now.

One of the wounded sailors recognized Alexander even though he was close to fainting from his wounds. He was one of the few service men who made an effort of knowing the Baranoffs and their son. He knew what had happened to Alexander's parents.

"How are you doing, kid?"

Alexander shrugged his shoulders and tried unsuccessfully to smile.

The sailor replied, "Keep a stiff upper lip. You'll be all right."

Alexander acknowledged the sentiment and quickly responded, "Do you know where we are headed?"

"I couldn't tell you, but I'd be willing to bet that we are headed for Anchorage or Kodiak Island."

Alexander frowned and turned his head towards the windows,

seeking answers through his eyes. The names mentioned had no meaning to him.

The sailor grinned and said, "Well, I'm really not sure where we are headed, but I'm sure the pilot might give you a better idea where we are going than I would."

Alexander had not been told specifically where he was being taken, but he speculated that he was headed for a destination somewhere in the interior of Alaska just to the northeast. Pouting, he sat back against the curved fuselage, still aching in his heart for his dead parents.

Just as the plane lifted off despite the difficulties presented by the water, a single Japanese Zero appeared off to the southern horizon.

"Bogie at five o'clock," Alexander heard the co-pilot exclaim. "Let's get out of here and head her into a cloud bank."

The Zero, approaching from a distance, appeared to be headed for the PBY, but just as it appeared as if the Japanese pilot had drawn a bead on the Catalina, cloud cover enveloped the fuselage of the American plane.

It wouldn't keep the PBY hidden for long. The cloud cover was sparse.

CHAPTER 9

"Blast it!" exclaimed the pilot. "Where did that Nip come from?"

The co-pilot frantically scanned the air space behind the Catalina. The cloud cover had broken. "Forget that right now. He spotted us. Lieutenant! For God's sake, get us out of here! There's no way that he can miss us. The cloud cover is gone. Look out! He's right behind us!"

The pilot turned the controls trying the impossible, to out maneuver a Japanese Zero with an old PBY. "Matt, hurry it up. Take your pistol and shoot at that meatball. Get him off my tail!"

The co-pilot unholstered his 45 and opened the cockpit window, trying to get a shot off against the faster plane. Alexander could see from his position in the back of the plane that the Zero was well in position to make a killing.

"Get down, you fool!" one of the men in the side booth shouted at him.

Alexander understood completely that it really didn't matter if he were up or down. It was more than likely that he would die in the same manner that his parents were killed. He watched through the back canopy as the guns of the Japanese plane started blazing.

Alexander instinctively ducked and heard machine gun bullets angrily clicked against the fuselage as they hit the PBY. The Zero flew by.

"Alexander, get up here quickly!" yelled the pilot. "Matt's been hit. You need to take the gun away from him."

Alexander grimaced as he made his way towards the cockpit. The co-pilot's head hung limp to the side, a bloody quarter inch hole in his temple. A large gray pistol was still clutched in his hand, but it had not been fired. The co-pilot apparently had just stuck his pistol out of the window to shoot when he was struck in the head by the Japanese's bullet.

Alexander quickly pried the 45 out of the dead man's hand and pointed it out the side sliding of the canopy. The young Russian struggled momentarily to hold on to the gun as the wind nearly ripped it out of his cold grasp.

"Hold on to it!" shouted the pilot. "Our nasty little Nippon friend is coming back."

Alexander peered out into the partially cloudy sky. The Zero was coming in again from the port side of the Catalina. Alexander trembled as he leveled the pistol at the on-coming plane. He steadied the gun even as the guns of the Zero flashed out directly at him with bright orange streaks. Alexander squeezed the trigger once and then twice. The propeller on the Zero sputtered to a stop. Alexander could see the pilot of the Zero as he streaked by. It appeared that the Japanese pilot was clutching his right shoulder near the throat. As he flashed by, Alexander could swear he could see blood blotted on the throat of the pilot.

The young Russian glanced apprehensively at the weapon in his hand. He had never handled a gun before, especially one like this that looked light, but was deceptively heavy. Alexander nervously shook in that brief second that he held the gun, but was convinced that he had hit the pilot. "You may not believe this but there was blood where he was holding his shoulder. I shot him. I really shot him." Alexander looked over the head of American pilot where he could now see the Zero drifting harmlessly away.

"I don't know if you did or didn't," the pilot skeptically countered, "…but I hope you're right. I'll just keep my eye on him."

The young Russian could feel his hand trembling as he watched the Japanese plane drift away from the Catalina. He noticed the dubious looks of every passenger's face on board the plane. Alexander felt indignant to explain what really happened. "I am sure I hit him." He turned to the pilot. "You can see for yourself that he is not coming back."

The pilot nodded his head. Out of his cockpit port window, he could see that the deadly plane was headed away from its intended prey. The Zero was just barely holding its own just above the waves of the surf. In the far distance, the small chain of the Aleutian islands could be seen. The pilot would try to land on one of these small windy atolls if he were wounded. The pilot could tell the way the plane was holding up that the Jap would probably make it. "You're right, kid. He is not coming back. You probably did hit him. Well, let's not stick around and find out."

Alexander had every reason to gloat, but his thoughts were directed towards the Japanese pilot and the possibility of revenge. The young Russian silently wished that his newest enemy would die a horrible death. Alexander remembered what had taken place at Dutch Harbor. The sailors had taught him some slang and he thought one was appropriate now. "I hope you burn in hell," he muttered under his breath. Alexander shook his head at what he just suggested. "That is an American saying. The Russian people do not believe in hell or a heaven. I have been around these Americans much too long." Still angry, the Russian looked once more at the Zero that was now nearly out of sight. "Voshvodoniah, seebah sah-bah-kah!" (*Goodbye, you dog!*)

It was forty minutes later when Alexander finally relaxed enough to move from his seat next to the pilot, back to the passenger compartment.

"One of the wounded sailors struggled to sit up. "Well, what did the pilot say? Where are we going?"

"I tried everything to get it out of him. He won't tell me."

"Considering what you just did, I'm sure you can get him to change his mind. Give it another shot."

Alexander nodded his head and with determination, he made his way back into the cockpit. He squatted behind the pilot and tapped him on the shoulder.

The pilot took off his headset and turned around. "Yeah, what do you want?"

"I want to know where we are going." Alexander pleaded with his eyes. "Please, sir?"

The pilot frowned for a second and then said, "Well, I'm really not supposed to tell you, you know, just in case the Japs find us, but I guess it will be okay. I don't think that we'll be ambushed this close to the main land or this far north. The Japanese fleet is south of us." The pilot turned around once again to face forward, but snickered as he spoke. "I'm talking to myself now. I think I will fly to Soldotna." With a sarcastic smile the pilot whispered out loud, "I hope nobody heard that."

Alexander laughed under his breath and went back to his seat. He didn't know where Soldotna[1] was located, but it had a nice Russian name.

The Catalina flew northeast along the southern coastline of Alaska. There were no more encounters with unfriendly forces. Alexander could clearly see the lush green forests of Sitka Spruce and the white coastal mountains far below. When it was safe to finally tell everyone why they were going to Soldotna, it was then that Alexander learned that he would be temporarily staying with a family in that town until it was safe for him to return to the Soviet Union. Unfortunately, every military leader assumed that the Japanese would soon attack the Aleutians and maybe even invade the Islands. If they were successful, the Japanese Empire would control the major route to the Soviet Union.

There was an added complication because of the secrecy associated with the mission that Alexander's father was trying to accomplish. The Americans would suffer a demoralizing setback in their relations with the Soviets if Alexander were to fall into the hands of the Japanese. If captured, Alexander could reveal much of the operational phase of the lend-lease program and could divulge other information that could be useful to the Axis powers. The Japanese in all likelihood would question the young man if they got a hold of him and then would hand him over to the Nazis.

---

1 Soldotna is "Soldier" in Russian

With their new-found knowledge of the lend-lease routes, the Nazis would increase their zeal to reach Alaska and have the advantage of knowing where to strike.

Back at Dutch Harbor, decisions were being made that would affect the young man from Russia. Captain Updegraff watched the skies uneasily. The first attack on Dutch Harbor was devastating. There was every conceivable possibility that the Japanese would strike again. The captain detected some motion behind him and he quickly laid the binoculars on his chest. General Butler was coming up the pathway towards him, followed by two orderlies. Updegraff snapped a quick salute to his superior. The general returned it.

"Do you really think they'd have the nerve to strike us again?"

"Yes sir, I do. We'll be ready for them this time, I assure you."

"Good. By the way, were all the civilians transported to the mainland?"

"Yes sir!"

"Including the Russian ambassador's son?"

"Yes sir."

"Good. Well, we know for certain that he can't go home the same way he arrived. He is to remain in Soldotna as long as the present conditions remain. Is that to be understood, captain?"

"Yes sir and I totally agree. He will remain on the Kenai Peninsula."

The captain turned to a nearby aide and scribbled down some lines on a small circular-wired note pad. "Send this dispatch immediately to Major Hunt in the town of Soldotna on the mainland of Alaska."

Private Richardson looked briefly at the scrawled note and dropped his jaw. "But sir, the Russian won't understand if we try to force him to stay. He wants to go home."

The captain turned beet red. "The lad can't go home. Communications and sea lanes have been cut between the Soviet Union and us. The Japs might get a hold of him if we try to send him home. Is that what you want to happen, soldier?" the captain bellowed in irritated anger. "Blast it, soldier, I don't like it any more than you do, but these are orders from General Butler. Your job is to make sure that they are carried out. Now go send it."

"Yes sir!"

The private looked despondently at the slip of paper in his hand. He knew that the young Russian didn't want to be forcefully torn from his homeland. He understood a little bit how Alexander would feel when he received this note. Referring to his southern upbringing, the private declared, "He'll be madder than a wet hen before Sunday dinner."

CHAPTER 10

Alexander surveyed the green coastline of Alaska down below him as the Catalina plane dropped in elevation. Green spruce trees carpeted the pinnacles and valleys that pivoted down to the blue-green waters of the Pacific. "What a stunning place."

The young man suddenly remembered his Russian teaching. "America cannot be this beautiful. This is impossible, but it must be real." He began to think of all the possibilities of such a lush green land. "I could sure use this—a new land, maybe a new life, possibly away from all my trouble."

Alexander was trying to imagine how his life would change where he was going. He wondered about the residents and Soldotna itself. "So what's this town like?" he asked the pilot. "How do you know so much about it?"

The pilot reached down beside his seat to check some charts without turning to his Russian passenger. "Well, you might say I was stationed there for a short while. It's your typical small American town—a gas station, a small greasy spoon restaurant, and a post office. Soldotna isn't all that far from the huge metropolis of Anchorage, where a large contingent of army troops were stationed when I was here the last time. Soldotna, in fact, is about 150 miles from Anchorage, the largest city in Alaska. That driving distance refers to the route along the western shore of the Kenai Peninsula. If you went by way of the ocean route in a ship, it is much shorter, only 65 miles across the Cook Inlet."

The pilot looked back. "Of course, kid, you still didn't hear any of that and if you did I want you to forget anything you heard. It would be bad for our boys over here if any of that information leaks out. Do I make myself clear?"

"Uhh, yes sir!"

The pilot brought his radio microphone up to his mouth. "Strawberry 16 reporting. We are 30 miles due south of Salmon 4. We had an encounter with a bogie two hours ago. I have three wounded and one dead. Request landing instructions. Over."

"Stand by, Strawberry 16. Awaiting confirmation of your aircraft."

Two minutes went by when the radio operator came back. "Strawberry 16, land your craft at dock just west of objective. Over."

"Roger."

"What is Salmon 4?" asked Alexander.

"That's the town of Kenai. We are landing there."

"So, where is Soldotna?"

"It's a few miles east of where we are landing."

"So, you know all about this town of Soldotna. Can you tell me any more about it?"

The pilot adjusted himself in the seat and gazed quickly to the side and back without turning his head, "Well, let me tell you. Soldotna is a small community, but it is home to some of the army troops preparing to work on the Alaskan Highway. That's a road the Canadians and Americans are building north out of the United States into Alaska. The major, whom you will meet shortly, was in charge of part of a construction detail there until he transferred to the air corps. It is at Soldotna that the army believes you will be safe for the time being. It is far enough inland that if the Japanese did invade Alaska, then they think you could be moved without too much indication of your location from the shore. They thought an army man would be the best for the job. So they decided that you, my young friend, would be left in the care of Major Thomas Brendan Hunt of the Army Air Corps. Major Hunt is a soldier who resides in Soldotna and he has worked with intelligence before. Therefore, they know that he can be entrusted with the safe-keeping of a young Russian lad like yourself."

The pilot confided in Alexander that he wouldn't be lonely during his stay with the family. "You see, the major has five children. I'm trying to remember them from the meeting I had with him eight months ago. What are their names? Ah, let's see. There are the twins, Jeremy and Carrie. They are four years old. Their newest addition is Timothy. He is two. Another boy, Christopher, is nine, and oh yeah, the oldest I think is Brenda. She is thirteen, I believe." The pilot scrunched his brow. "And the major's wife is... Susan. That's the family you'll be staying with."

"I suppose they're all capitalists," Alexander pouted. "I don't think I will like it there."

"Don't knock it until you try it," the captain indignantly responded with a grin.

"Well, I guess I don't have much choice in the matter, do I?"

"No, I guess you don't." The pilot looked Alexander straight in the eye. "Now Alexander, you must realize that you must avoid strangers in this town and for a little while try to stay out of sight as much as possible, until we know that it is safe for you to come out of hiding. There is not much of a chance that Axis agents are working in this area, but we want to make sure that you are safe. Do you understand?"

"Yeah," he came back with a sad reply.

The Catalina soon came to a beautiful greenish-blue inlet. The young Russian could see that a small wooden dock near the water was loaded with people.

The plane descended and the pilot cut power as he prepared to land on the water near the wooden dock near a couple of fishing boats. The buildings of the town were small. Most were one story fabrications.

"Is this part of the ocean?" Alexander asked.

"This is part of the Cook Inlet," the pilot replied. "That is Soldotna over there beyond the town of Kenai." The pilot pointed to a wide stretch of trees in the direction of the eastern horizon. The tower of a church could barely be seen above the top of the forest.

Alexander could feel a great deal of nervousness in the pit of his stomach. Everything was so strange and all these events had happened too fast. He closed his eyes and put his hand over his navel trying to hold it steady as the plane descended.

The plane roared into the docking area where Alexander saw people lined up on the wharf. A number of ambulances and cars were also lined up on the dock area. Some were for the wounded. One was reserved for the dead co-pilot. Alexander was quickly briefed on the type of role he should play until it was time for him to return to the Soviet Union. He was not to go away from the town by himself for any reason. The young Russian was told not to divulge any information about the base at Dutch Harbor to anyone or relay any information about his father's mission.

The pilot reached for controls over his head. "Alexander, I know this is all too much to take in right away, but anything you say about what happened could jeopardize the war for both your country and ours. Please try to stay inconspicuous. Please be patient and stay out of trouble. You need to wait because there are no other safe alternatives right now. If anything were to happen to you, it might just well create an international incident between Russia and the United States. Above all stay out of the hands of the Japanese and the Nazis. It was bad enough that two Russian nationalists were killed on American soil while on a secret mission, but if you were killed or captured, I hate to think what devastating effect it would have for the future."

"Okay, okay. I will stay with this family for a while and I'll try to keep out of trouble."

Alexander looked out the window of the plane as it spluttered up to the docking area. Some curious fishermen and a few of the townspeople were there, trying to figure out what in the world a military transport plane and three ambulances were doing there. Alexander could see from his vantage point that the crowd of curious people was growing.

From out of the group came a family of four children and two adults. They were apparently the ones that would take the young refugee into their home. The man was a tall individual, even taller than his own father. He had a clean-shaven face and a muscular body. Major Hunt wore a trim green army uniform on and his hair was short and nicely trimmed. The major appeared to be in his late thirties. His wife was about the same age with pretty auburn hair that came down to her shoulders. She had a nylon wrap around the back part of the hair with a small frontal bun on her forehead. This was explained to the young Russian as the latest rave and style for American women. Her smile provided Alexander a temporary relief of happiness. He could see that the children respected her.

Christopher, the oldest boy, stood alone away from the others. His nine-year-old frame was tall and slender for his age. He stepped forward even after his mother had asked him to step back away from the plane. "He's the courageous one of the lot," Alexander surmised. The boy's demeanor showed a type of independence that the others had not shown. His independent streak showed the young Russian that this boy was one to be a handful for his parents at times. He wore an old blue collar buttoned up shirt with short sleeves and blue jeans. He was the one that could relate to Alexander the most, as he stood by himself.

The four-year-old twins stood nearby as they looked at the Catalina with wide eyes. The young girl hid behind her mother while the slightly freckled brown-haired boy stood out a little. They wore red and white t-shirts and blue jeans. Their rambunctious behavior began to taper down as the door of the Catalina opened. Alexander cautiously stepped out of the airplane unto the dock.

The children eyed him with great curiosity. Alexander felt ill at ease as he stepped away from the safe haven of the Catalina flying boat. Major Hunt in his handsome brown uniform, held the youngest child Timothy, in his arms. The boy kept switching positions with his head, trying to take in all the activity.

Alexander peered at the others in the gathering. Among the crowd were two teenage boys, Paul Grayson and Craig Reynolds. These young men had heard of the young foreigner and had come down to see what their new classmate would be like.

Alexander surmised that they were trying to judge him by his appearance to see if he were dressed differently than other people. Some sense of distrust of a foreigner undoubtedly came from the reality of war. Alexander could understand and identify with this type of reasoning. Everyone, with the exception of the Hunts, was nervous.

Alexander hardly recognized the existence of the four-year old twins or the oldest boy. His eyes focused almost immediately on the oldest girl, Brenda, who stayed near two of her classmates. She was quite pretty, even for being an American. Her long silky auburn hair ran past her shoulders and her deep dark brown eyes sparkled like the nearby waters of the Inlet. Her bright eyes flashed towards the plane in fascination and wonderment. Her smile even out-dazzled her mother's. She was slender, about the same height as Alexander.

Standing with Brenda were two of her closest friends, Lori and Jennifer. They had an immediate reaction to the young Russian boy. "He's pretty cute," Lori swooned. "You're quite the lucky girl. Imagine, having him stay at your house."

"He's okay, I guess," Brenda remarked, trying to get a reaction. In reality, she couldn't help but admire the sleek young Russian youth, but she was not about to let on that she thought he was handsome.

"Okay! I would say so." rebuked Lori.

"Well, maybe he is sort of cute."

Jennifer jumped in. "Cute nothing—he's more than that. He's gorgeous."

Brenda countered, "Possibly, but he is Russian. I don't plan to be around him all that much."

"Good," Lori replied. "I'll be over a lot and take care of him for you." The girls all laughed.

"Hello, Alexander!" called out Mrs. Hunt, who had already guessed that this young man was her newest boarder. She held out her hand. "I'm Susan Hunt."

Alexander smiled slightly. He could tell by the tone in her voice that Mrs. Hunt was a genuinely very nice woman. The calmness and gentleness in her voice immediately put the young Russian at ease. It was apparent right away that the charms of this American woman would help Alexander adjust quickly to his new surroundings.

Major Hunt walked up. "Hello, Alexander. I'm Major Brendan Hunt and this is Timothy." Timothy seemed motionless in the major's arms as he stared at the young Russian.

"Hello." Alexander nervously muttered as they ushered him to an awaiting car. "Is this the point of no turning back?" The young Russian halfway believed that he would end up in some American jail. "Is this family just pretending to be nice? Is this just a ruse to get me inside the car?"

Suddenly a few of the spectators gathered near the dock, simultaneously turned their faces towards the plane as two men came out carrying a stretcher with the body of the co-pilot on it.

Alexander cringed as he watched the limp body go by him. A bleached-white hand dangled from beneath the sheet. Alexander put his hand up to his mouth and turned sharply away. He was sick of death.

Susan Hunt saw his reaction to the body and went to comfort him. *This boy needs a lot of love,* she thought privately.

Still in a somewhat state of shock, Alexander let Mrs. Hunt hold him as they made their way to the family sedan. The rest of the family crowded in.

Complete adjustment would take Alexander a long time, but the entire Hunt household grew to like the young man from Russia immensely. Alexander was an instant hit with the Hunt family, but Mr. and Mrs. Hunt wondered how the rest of the American community would accept him.

Alexander had the same concerns. There was a certain amount of distrust in some of the eyes of the villagers watching him. There was a war going on and this fact reflected to a natural fear of foreigners.

The young man decided to make it a point that he would try his best to get along with the people of Soldotna. He was tentative about getting in the vehicle with the family, but eventually he decided that there was nowhere else to go. He sat near the window, avoiding most of the conversation directed at him.

Back at the home of the Hunts, Alexander tried to shake off the images of the death of his parents. There was little hope in the endeavor. Every time he closed his eyes, the young Russian would visualize their death over and over. The vivid images would stay with him for years to come.

That night at the supper table the nervous young stranger sat down for his first American meal. He suspiciously eyed everything that was laid out before him. Everything was new and strange. It was definitely not a meal that he usually had back in Russia.

Mrs. Hunt tried her best to put the young man at ease. "Alexander, I want you to feel at home. If there is anything you need at all, you let us know, okay?"

"Sure. Mrs. Hunt, I do appreciate what you are doing. I'm sorry that I am so quiet, but a lot has happened to me today. I think I might still be a little shaky after the Japanese attack."

"We understand perfectly." Mrs. Hunt noticed the stares of her own children. "Children, it is rude to stare," she uttered softly.

Alexander politely held up his hand. "It is okay, Mrs. Hunt. I'm sure they are not accustomed to the idea of a stranger in their house."

"Just the same I want them to show some proper manners. We want you to feel completely at home here, Alexander. We will have no more of this type of behavior."

At this prompting, the kids slowly resumed eating their meal and tried hard not to notice their visitor, but many of the children continued to take unhindered sneak peeks towards their new visitor.

The oldest child was the worst of the perpetrators. Brenda was persistent in looking in the Russian boy's direction. She continued for a brief minute until she noticed that her father was glaring at her and clearing his throat. She took a quick bite, and looked up again at the Russian. *He is kind of cute,* she thought. Major Hunt saw a hint of a chuckle in his daughter's eyes. He quickly glanced uneasily at both his daughter and his young Russian ward.

Alexander rubbed his forehead gently with his free hand. Fatigue was settling into his eyes. The day had been a long one for the young boy. He asked Mrs. Hunt about where he could rest.

"It's upstairs, dear," she said as she walked him up.

They approached his door of his room. "Remember, Alexander, it's the second door on the right from the top of the stairs. I'll leave you alone, but I'll send up Brenda with some clean sheets."

"Thank you."

Alexander slowly trudged to the top of the stairs and opened the indicated door. Alexander surveyed his dwelling space trying to figure out how he wanted the chamber.

A single bed was lying in the corner with a single large window above it. This suited the young Russian fine for it faced into the western horizon where his home, Russia, lay beyond the Bering Strait. A slight musty odor penetrated his nostrils, indicating that the room had been vacated a long time ago.

There came a knock at the door. It was Brenda holding some folded bed sheets. "These are for you. We'll bring up the blankets later."

"Thanks," Alexander muttered.

Brenda laid out the sheet on his bed. She twitched her head to ask a question. "What is it like living in Russia?" she coyly asked, trying to get the young man to open up.

"Quite a bit different than living here," answered Alexander, his accent betraying his heritage. "I don't imagine you have had it as rough as I have had."

"Oh, I don't know. There is always the threat of an invasion from the Japanese."

"So it seems, or did you forget, my parents were just killed by the Japanese!" he replied in an irritated voice.

The facial features on Brenda's face tightened. "Hey, I didn't mean anything by it. I was just wondering what it was like to live in Russia!" Brenda blurted out. "You know I am just interested in your country. There's no need to get huffy."

Alexander took over the spreading of the sheet from Brenda. "I'm sorry if you misunderstood. I…I have had a rough time."

Brenda grabbed a corner of the sheet and tucked it in. Her eyes slowly drifted up to the young man. "Is it lonely for you here?"

Alexander sheepishly looked up at the young girl. "I'm sorry, but it has been very hard on me. I only wish to rest and I don't feel like talking too much right now."

Brenda tried to respond but just then her mother called up to her. "Brenda, come down and carry up these blankets and pillows." She made it sound as if she wanted Brenda to come down right away before anything happened. Alexander seemed to be a nice boy, but he was still a stranger for the time being. Brenda huffed and left, a little frustrated.

Alexander shook his head. He couldn't decide at first if the girl was interested in his life or if she was just trying to tease him because of his foreign status. He decided it would be better to avoid the impetuous young lady for as long as he could.

Soon the day had come to a peaceful end despite its violent beginning. The sun was setting in a spectacular red horizon as Alexander stared out into the western sky from his bedroom window. Brenda was right about one thing at that moment—he was a very lonely young man.

Despite his loneliness, Alexander was determined in his heart and mind not to get too involved with Americans, no matter how nice they were to him. They were neither his kind nor his countrymen.

The lonely young man could feel nothing but grief and he vowed in his heart to fulfill his mother's desire to be back in Russia. He was determined to go back to Dutch Harbor and take the bodies of his parents back to Russia. For the next few days, he would constantly ask about the possibilities of going back to Dutch Harbor while he was staying with the Hunts during the first few days after being brought to live with them.

Major Hunt kept reminding him, "We need to make sure it is all right with the war department. Don't worry. We will get you home."

Major Hunt liked the boy, but he was a little concerned with the possible affect this foreign boy might have on his oldest daughter. There were some initial warning signs already. He kept a close eye on both of them.

The next day, June 4, 1942
Dutch Harbor, the Aleutians

"Jake, get him!" screamed the auxiliary gunner as he fed the bullet casing into the machine gun. "You would think they would have better sense than to come back here."

"Why not?" retorted the gunner, yelling over the blasts of the machine gun. "They came close to destroying a lot of what we have here already. In fact, they pretty well creamed us."

True to what the sailor had said, the Japanese Zeroes had returned to wreck havoc on the army base at Dutch Harbor.

A bomb careened from one of the planes and pummeled into a nearby barrack. The building blossomed into a huge bright orange fireball.

"Bob, there's one coming in from the west. You got to stop him. He's after the ship."

The gunner swung his gun around sharply to try and knock down another Japanese plane that was diving towards the supply ship docked at the harbor.

It was too late for the ground gunners to react.

Both men watched as a single bomb plummeted towards what was left of the *Northwestern*. The bomb pierced the steel deck and a large sickening boom could be heard coming from inside her hull. Her sides buckled out on both sides as a huge explosion wracked the damaged ship with orange flames shooting out of the hatches like a huge blowtorch.

The men continued shooting at other targets, but one sailor summed it up after the explosion on the *Northwestern*. "They hit her again. One thing for sure, she'll never float again. So much for that poor kid getting back to Russia." He remembered how much trouble he had trying to get the lad into the PBY.

"What kid?" asked the sailor feeding the bullets to the gun.

"Don't you remember—the Russian?"

"Oh, yeah, that hard-headed scamp. You're right, it might be a long time before he gets back to Russia!"

CHAPTER 11

Back on the mainland, Major Hunt received the vital phone call that Alexander had hinged his hopes on for going home to Russia.

With great anticipation, Mrs. Hunt was standing next to him, trying to make out what the conversation was all about and listened to the side as her husband talked.

After hanging up, the major relayed the message to his wife. "The Japanese bombed Dutch Harbor again and completely destroyed the *Northwestern* along with all the military supplies in the Siem-Drake warehouse that were supposed to be taken to Vladivostok. Without the supplies and the ship, there is no need to take another risk so soon with our young Russian friend. The government decided that they should wait for a better opportunity to move Alexander back into his own country." He grimly put his hand to his chin. "We really don't have any choice but to keep him here for a while."

"Wouldn't he be able to go home by way of Nome?" his wife asked.

"No," he replied softly, "…because the Japanese have invaded two of the most western islands of the Aleutian chain, Kiska and Attu. They now control the sea-lanes between Alaska and Russia. With enemy forces in that area, it would be much too dangerous to move the boy back to his homeland." A slight smile came over his face. "There is some good news as well. The main Japanese fleet had lost four carriers near Midway Island. Some of our officers in the high command believe that means a very serious blow to the future invasion plans of the Empire of Japan. Some officers in the highest echelon of the army believe that the Japanese are now incapable of invading the mainland of Alaska." He cocked his head in nonchalant manner. "Despite the victory at Midway, they still say that it would be too dangerous to return any of the Russian nationals to their homeland. Alexander will have to stay here for the time being."

Without knowing the circumstances, the young Russian's fate had been decided for him.

Alexander would find out much later what had already been determined by people he hardly knew.

June 7, 1942

A naval attaché and his aide arrived at Soldotna four days after Alexander had been flown there. Before the Japanese raid on Dutch Harbor, it was decided that the young Russian would be brought back into his country on board the *Northwestern*. The Japanese made sure that this was no longer a possibility.

The naval officers removed their caps as Alexander appeared before them. Major Hunt brought his right hand down towards the officers in an introduction gesture. "Alexander, this is Captain Bliss and Lieutenant Evans. The lieutenant you have met before."

"Yes, it is good to see you again." Alexander went right to the main point of what he perceived to be the reason for the visitors. "When can I go home?" The statement was very blunt and very direct and made with a hint of a threat.

The two military men glanced at each other uneasily. Evans spoke first. "Alexander, it may not be possible for a long time. The Japanese have invaded Attu and Kiska in the western Aleutians. They control the main strait between your homeland and Alaska. We need you to stay here where it will be safe for just a little while longer. If the Japanese are defeated soon, we might be able to get you home at that time."

"Will you let me go home then?" The young Russian's suspicions mounted. Deep seeded Soviet indoctrination had taught him well about Russian citizens being forced to stay in the United States against their will.

Captain Bliss frowned for he knew what the boy was thinking. "That could be a long time, kid. The Japanese will not surrender without a long fight."

Alexander's eyes narrowed and his face contorted into a huge frown. "You will let me know when," he demanded.

Captain Bliss tried to reassure the young man. "The very minute that the war ends, you'll be the first to know."

Alexander, true to his anti-American sentiments, remained skeptical, but he decided there was nothing else to do presently, but to stay with the Hunts for the time being.

With this new source of unexpected information, Alexander calculated his alternatives and decided that he would bide his time and possibly escape later. He was well aware that there were no safe alternatives and it would create an international incident if he were killed.

Alexander was equally unaware that the United States military was under close scrutiny in aspect to the boy's well being. In Moscow, the general Soviet council did not believe in the answers they were given. Skeptical about the death of their Russian ambassador and his wife, the leaders of the Soviet regime perceived deception on the part of the Americans and their intentions for Alexander.

It was bad enough that two Russians were killed on American territory while on a secret mission, but a young Russian boy was being detained illegally by an ally. The Soviets were constantly questioning the American State Department on the manner in which Boris and Sonja were killed. There were huge suspicions on their part.

Adding to the trepidation were inaccurate rumors in the Kremlin that Boris was shot in the back by "friendly forces." It was decided by the more skeptical and radical men of the Soviet council that almost any accusation could be conjured to get young Alexander back to his homeland.

In any case, Alexander agreed with the Americans that waiting for the moment would be sufficient on a temporary basis. He promised to settle down with his provisional adopted family.

Two weeks later

When the time came to give out confidential information, the young Russian finally learned the awful truth about what had happened to the bodies of his parents. The attaché at first was reluctant to give all the full details, but Alexander was insistent that he be told everything.

"I am sorry, young man, but we could not bury them as Russians. Their graves were given different identities and they were buried as American civilian workers."

Alexander's face turned ashen gray with anger and despair, but he continued to listen.

Captain Bliss continued with his directive. "In order to keep your father's mission a secret from the Japanese, we had to bury them as American civilian workers. Your government has agreed to this to avoid public scrutiny. Alexander, you must understand. We had no choice."

Alexander felt complete derogation of what he had to endure. He had promised himself that the bodies of his parents were to be buried in Russia with their own names. Apparently the Americans were going to prevent this from happening.

Alexander reacted quickly with anger in his heart. "This is what is proper in a land of democracy? Who in this land cared about individual rights? I swear to you, that however long it takes; my parents will be given the proper recognition on their tombstones. I want an opportunity to return to Dutch Harbor some day."

The attaché bristled. "It will be after the danger from the Japanese has passed and not before."

Alexander scrunched his mouth in disgust and puffed out his chest to give him courage. "Very well! Understand this though, if the Japanese take over this country, I will still get to my parents somehow and changed their grave markers. At least you could afford me that dignity."

Captain Bliss nodded his head and shook Alexander's hand. His face was etched with consternation. "I wish you the best of luck. I really do." He turned and left.

"Yeah, thanks a lot," Alexander grumbled after the door had closed. "I hope some day I'll be able to get even with you Cossack capitalists, maybe after we destroy the Germans. As far as I'm concerned, my distrust of Americans is growing by leaps and bounds."

Over the next four days, Alexander's anger subsided to some extent. After the first initial and somewhat tense situation, Alexander found that adjusting to this new country and the people that lived there was fairly easy.

The Hunt family was a substantial reason for the character change in the young man from Russia. Alexander was quick to learn tolerance and soon was always on his best behavior.

After their initial encounter with Alexander, most of the people in the town considered the young Russian to be a decent young man. Alexander's personality even won over some of the townspeople in Soldotna that despised foreigners. Many respected the major and his wife and the Hunts were treating Alexander like he was part of the family.

Eventually Alexander could feel an increasing sense of what it was like to be an American with the help of the Hunts and his new friends at school.

Alexander learned as well that the charm he admired so much in Mrs. Hunt ran in the family. Everyone in the Hunt clan welcomed him with open arms just like a big brother. This included the somewhat shy but beautiful thirteen-year-old Brenda Hunt. This young lady was no ordinary teenage girl. She was slender like her mom with the same long wavy auburn hair that flowed down just beyond her shoulders. The many curls that bounced with her every step enhanced her hair. Brenda's eyes sparkled just like her mother's eyes and they were full of fire and laughter all at the same time. They were warm and inviting as well. There was something special about her that made her stand out from the other young people in town. Brenda was extremely intelligent for her age and she knew how to use her charm in detracting Alexander.

Brenda started off being friends with the young man and would often talk to Alexander about the differences between the United States and the Soviet Union. "What is it like over there?" she would often ask. Alexander's answers were not always things that Brenda cared to hear.

After he figured out that Brenda was trying to irritate him at one point, Alexander decided to be blunt with her. "We have the greatest people in the world. Our country is strong with people who are not cowards, not like the weaklings and capitalists that live in this land."

Brenda bristled. "How dare you! Our people are just as strong as your people, if not better. Democracy is much better than communism. Are you so blind that you can't see that in many ways the Russians are just as bad as the Nazis?"

Brenda could see that anger was swelling in the heart of the young man from the Soviet Union as he glared at her, furiously. "I'm sorry. I didn't mean it to quite come out that way, but isn't Marxism based on taking over the other economies of the other countries."

Alexander glowered at the young lady who was just trying to tease him, but managed finally to nod. "It is the only way for every one to have an equal opportunity."

Brenda set her gaze upon his face, trying to outwit him. "But other countries are not willing to adapt that system. Lenin and Stalin have both stated the only way to get people to change their economics was to take over their countries and force communism on them. In that sense, I see little difference from what the Nazis are trying to accomplish—no difference at all."

Alexander put his fist into his open palm. "And what do you know. All you have been taught is to be anti anything that is contrary to the morals of your country," Alexander snapped back angrily. "I think the best thing for both of us is to ignore the subject of politics as long as I am here. Hopefully that will not be too long."

"Fine with me—and it can't be too soon as far as I am concerned," Brenda quipped and abruptly turned her face away from Alexander

Brenda took one more defiant glare in Alexander's direction. She then turned and burst out of the room. "Some nerve," she spouted to herself, "…and here I thought he was cute." She bounded down the hallway. She grinned. "Well, I can't fault him for that."

CHAPTER 12

August 1942, Soldotna

Alexander could not have imagined how different Soldotna was from either Leningrad or Unalaska, but he was learning about the major differences quickly. The beauty of the land was different in itself and there was a sense of friendliness that he had not experienced for a long time except from his parents. He had adjusted quickly to the Alaskans and the land.

Of course, there were people close to his own age that were interested in his Russian heritage. This was a huge factor for Alexander's influence in this new land. With his own delightful personality, Alexander made friends quickly with some of the boys around town.

There were also some who despised Alexander just because he was a foreigner. One of these young men was a bulky individual that had developed into a natural bully. His name was Harrison Fisher.

Harrison was a young man whose main attribute was his boasting ability. Husky and strong, he used his strength for his own purposes. His piercing blue eyes often displayed hate and distrust among most of the residents of Soldotna.

Harrison was one that expected much out of life, but did very little to gain it except by bullying people. He wasn't particularly tall, but he had a fairly large chest for his age. As soon as he could, Harrison grew a reddish-blonde bristly beard to add to his intimidation mystique. With few friends in his inner circle, Harrison was a boy who distrusted anyone different from himself. He manipulated those close to him and he used that power to the best of his ability. He expected much out of the world and his basic philosophy was,

"My way or no way."

Harrison's unscrupulous father had much to do with his son's attitude. A constant failure at different business ventures, his blame was directed at his son. When Harrison's mother died seven years earlier, Harrison's relationship with his father deteriorated even further. Mr. Fisher usually would only communicate with his son when he wanted something done for his own benefit.

One aspect of Harrison that most people admired was his handsome features. His hair was curly blonde which stood two inches above his scalp; also he was tall in stature. He was nearly a head taller than most of the boys his age. His deep blue eyes might have been considered hypnotizing and nice in most cases, but anyone could tell they were full of hate. His brutality was widely known by the peers of his school, especially the weaker ones. In each case when Harrison intimidated people younger and smaller than himself, he managed to just stay out of trouble either by threatening or making it appear as his victim was the aggressor. He had a knack for avoiding the obvious.

In addition, Harrison's vanity was second to none in Soldotna. Harrison, in his view, considered himself a complete ladies' man. He was notorious in Soldotna for his coercion tactics and unsavory advances towards the single women of the town, even women five years his senior.

One of Harrison's favorite strategies of getting girls to notice him was to block the sidewalk to slow their advance. His preferred object of attraction was Brenda Hunt. It was in the early spring of 1943 when he decided to get Brenda to go on a forced date with him. He had been upset with the presence of the Russian boy in the Hunt household and he was determined to change the admired status of Alexander somehow. Harrison had continued ridiculing Alexander several times behind his back and he wanted to curtail the apparent influence the young Russian was having on Brenda.

It came to a head one afternoon on the main street of Soldotna. Harrison intentionally blocked the path of Alexander and Brenda as they were window shopping near Mykel's, one of the local restaurants.

Harrison purposely ignored Alexander and directed his comments to Brenda. "Hey Brenda, see you at the dance?"

Brenda responded by ignoring him.

Harrison noticed the snub. He put his hand on her shoulder and responded, "I'll be expecting at least six dances with you and even something else after the dance."

Brenda grimaced and pushed his arm away. "In your dreams, jerk."

Alexander clenched his fist, but Brenda's quick look stopped him from reacting.

Harrison's sneer turned nasty. "Really, hon, I'm really not that bad of a person."

Brenda pulled Alexander's arm and maneuvered around the burly, rude teenager. "Get out of our way. We have things to do."

Harrison was about to press the matter, but some of the more concerned men of the town were watching him. He backed off and let the couple go.

Out of earshot of the big brute, Alexander bent down to whisper to Brenda, "Does that guy like you?" Alexander asked as they continue to abruptly walk away.

"I guess so, not that I care. He bugs me to go out with him every once in a while."

Alexander smiled when he heard the word, "bugs". He knew that Brenda didn't care for at least one guy. He was halfway hoping that she might like someone else better. They left the bully fuming because he had not received what he considered a satisfactory answer.

The two teenagers were halfway home when Brenda suddenly turned her right foot sideways and cried out, "I twisted my ankle!"

Alexander looked down at it. "It doesn't look too bad."

Brenda frowned. "But it hurts. Could you help me home?"

Alexander glanced sideways. "Okay. Here, lean on me."

Brenda's soft touch upon him sent some new, unique and wonderful feelings throughout his body as Brenda leaned into him. It was as if something special had taken place. He carefully and tenderly walked her to her house.

As they arrived at the house, Major Hunt came out and noticed right away how Brenda was gingerly leaning on Alexander. "Are you okay, Brenda?"

"Yes, it's just a twisted ankle."

She smiled at Alexander. "Thank you for seeing that I made it home."

Major Hunt was just as quick to notice how his daughter catered to the young Russian. He could also see the changes that had taken place in the last eight months between Alexander and his daughter. Her eyes had become more bright and lively when each was in the presence of the other. The major could see in his daughter's smile and beautiful eyes that she tremendously enjoyed the company of the young Russian.

"You better get upstairs and take care of that ankle." The major sensed alarm in his tightening throat. "I'll be up to check on your ankle later."

The budding relationship between his daughter and the Russian was even more evident later on that night when Major Hunt had a chance to talk to his daughter alone. The major thought he could confirm his suspicions.

Alexander, in the meantime, had slipped out of the house and was sitting out of sight of the back porch, lying on his back on the grass and gazing at the bright stars up above him in the cloudless sky.

Major Hunt didn't want to be overheard in the house and he led Brenda out to the back porch. It was a warm night and sat down with her on the porch.

Alexander was hidden around the corner and he could hear the major coming out. He decided not to disturb the man and his daughter, so he remained motionless, unaware of what was about to transpire.

With his hand stroking his chin, Major Hunt asked his daughter,

"What do you think about our young Russian friend?"

Brenda looked at the sidewalk in an attempt to hide her feelings. "He's okay, I guess," she replied with a hint of a smile on her face.

Major Hunt tried to reply kindly, but it was a curt response that came out of his mouth. "Sweetheart, I don't want to alarm you, but just try your best to stay clear of Alexander when you're alone."

Brenda frowned unable to comprehend her father's distrust. "But why?"

The major stammered as he glanced uneasily behind his shoulder towards the house where he assumed Alexander was still inside. "We just don't know that much about him and he is from a country that doesn't care for our government."

"But Father, he's not bad."

"I know it," Major Hunt turned down his lower lip in displeasure. This speech was harder than he imagined. "Just learn not to get close to him."

Brenda gave her father a somewhat stubborn pouting face. "But Alexander has been here almost a year. He has never done anything to harm me. Can't you consider that?"

Major Hunt began wringing his hands together nervously. "Well, yes," He stood up. "… but just don't get too close to him. That's all I'm asking."

Brenda looked up with imploring eyes. "I can still be friends with him, can't I?" Brenda gave her a father a puzzling look.

Major Hunt softened his stance. "Of course, sweetheart, you can always be friends with him. You can even write him when he returns to the Soviet Union."

Brenda gasped at the thought. The idea that her Russian friend would leave made her wince. There was sadness in the very notion that Alexander would go back home. The major could see it in her sparkling eyes.

With that remark, the major and his daughter went back inside the house, not knowing that Alexander had heard every word of their conversation from his hidden spot on the grass. He had genuinely listened unintentionally to what the major and his daughter had been talking about around the corner of the house and now he was sorry for what he had heard.

"Americans," he muttered. "I knew all along that I wasn't needed here and I don't belong here. I need to get out of this country some how."

He meditated on his possibilities for a moment. "Craig." He was thinking of one of the boys that had befriended him at school. He brightened as a new idea came to him. "Craig. I'll talk to him. He seemed to be a good enough of a chap. He will help me get out of this idiotic country."

Alexander quietly slipped back into the house and ran up to his room, trying to avoid the members of the Hunt household who were gathered in the living room around the radio, listening to some show called Amos and Andy.

He quickly gathered his meager belongings and put on a heavy coat. Avoiding the Hunts once again, Alex made a beeline out of the back door of the house towards Craig's house.

Arriving at the Reynolds' house, Alexander rapped softly at the door. It was Craig that answered. "Hey, Alexander," he looked at the bag in Alexander's hand, "are you going somewhere?"

Alexander looked with disdain at his anticipated deception. "Craig, I need to leave, but I need your help."

"Help doing what?" Craig looked at Alexander's bundle in his hand and suspected what Alexander wanted to do. "What do you want me to do?"

"Help me get away."

"Help you get away to where?"

Alexander briskly replied, "To Russia, of course."

"Are you nuts?" Craig implored Alexander to change his mind. "Alexander, do you know what you are doing?" Craig asked, trying to discourage Alexander with the irritated tone of his voice.

"Keep your voice down." Alexander peered anxiously into the house, hoping no one had over heard his plea. "No, I'm not nuts."

Alexander, with a twinge of guilt on his face, braced himself. "I...I need your help in convincing your father that I am heading back to Russia on a ship that is docked at Anchorage."

"How am I supposed to do that? He will ask why the Hunts are not taking you."

"That is why I came to you. Can you help me figure something out?"

Craig sighed. "Yeah, I suppose so. Do you have some idea or a plan?"

"Yeah." Alexander held up an official-looking piece of paper. "I need you to type a message to me on this official looking document, informing me that my relatives have agreed to take me back to the Soviet Union tonight?"

His look of anguish made Craig give in. He placed his hand on Alexander's shoulder. "The Hunts, have you thought about them?"

Alexander looked down to hide his shame. "I thought about them a lot, but it doesn't matter now anyway. I am just a burden to them."

Craig interjected. "What about my father? Do you have a good enough of a story made up in case he asks why the Hunts can't take you?"

"I thought of that. At the last minute I'll say to your father that their car broke down."

"He will ask why they are not with you now."

"I will simply tell them that I said all my goodbyes already and I am under a tight time restraint before the ship up in Anchorage leaves."

"You have all that figured out, do you?"

"Yeah. Now let's get that message typed up so I can get out of here."

Craig hesitated.

Alexander could see that he was stalling for time. "Come on, you big chicken. You want me to get home to my relatives, don't you?"

Craig stopped and shrugged his shoulders. "I suppose, but it's too bad. I think you and I could have been great friends."

Alexander nodded slightly. "Yeah, I think so too."

The two boys stepped into the house and went into the den. Craig began to type out a fake cable gram. After numerous mistakes and retyping, they finally came up with an authentic looking text.

The fake cablegram read:

```
To Alexander Baranoff
  Soldotna, Alaska
From Uncle Marco Baranoff
I am aboard the Sminoff, a freighter
lying in port at Anchorage at Pier
17. I am prepared to take you back
home, provided you can get to Anchor-
age before 9:00 P.M. on Friday the
18th of August, 1942. The ship will
set sail at that time. I am anxious
to see you once again.
Sincerely, Uncle Marco
```

Finding an official-looking envelope, the boys folded the message carefully and slid it inside.

"Well, here goes nothing," Craig nervously whispered. He opened the living room door and rolled his eyes.

The boys apprehensively headed into the living room and handed their fabrication to Mr. Reynolds, who was listening to Amos and Andy on the radio.

Craig's father studied the boys' faces intently as he read the message. His hand came up to his chin and his eyes focused intently on Alexander's eyes.

Alexander bit his bottom lip. His face was etched with apprehension. *He is not going to believe us! I'll never get home,* he thought.

CHAPTER 13

Back at the house of Major Hunt, no one had yet realized that their young Russian visitor had left in his quest to get back to the Soviet Union. Dinner was being served in the main dining room and Mrs. Hunt came in finishing up the trimming of the main meal. She carried the ham into the dining room where everyone was sitting with one exception.

Amidst the constant commotion of the large family, Alexander had been momentarily forgotten. The exception was Brenda who scanned the immediate vicinity of the house for the Russian lad. She was momentarily distracted by some motion to the side. The twins were squirming and everyone else was talking with someone else. It took Mrs. Hunt a little while to get everyone to settle down, adding to the momentary confusion.

Glancing around the table, it finally dawned on Mrs. Hunt that all her children were at the table, but someone was missing. She assumed that her young ward was still up in his room.

Mrs. Hunt turned to her eldest son. "Chris, could you go up and tell Alexander that it's time for supper."

Christopher sprang from his chair. "Sure, Mama."

The young boy walked smartly up the stairs. He was actually proud to do this task for he had grown fond of the new visitor. Christopher, in the short time he had been acquainted with Alexander, looked upon him like a big brother. He liked the Russian's independent nature and strength. He tried to model himself after Alexander even though his father had tried to discourage his son from becoming too close to the foreigner as he did with all his children, especially his oldest daughter. Christopher had it set in his mind that Alexander would somehow really take pleasure in America and they would be great buddies forever. He secretly hoped that Alexander would find a way to stay in Alaska.

Christopher bounded up the stairs and walked slowly to Alexander's door. It was curiously quiet. There was no indication of movement coming from behind the closed door. He rapped gently at the door.

"Alexander, its time to come down and eat."

There was no answer. Christopher knocked a little harder once again on the door. "Alexander, are you sleeping?" The aroma of the ham downstairs was beckoning Christopher downstairs. He couldn't understand why Alexander had not been drawn by the smell of the meal.

Bewildered, Christopher opened the door. No one was inside. Christopher failed to see that there were none of Alexander's belongings in the room. Christopher scratched his temple and went downstairs.

Mrs. Hunt was the first to notice that only one boy came down. "So, where is he?"

Mr. Hunt and the rest of the children stopped eating and looked over to Christopher. Silence filled the room.

Christopher shook his head. "I don't know, Mama, he's not up there."

Mrs. Hunt held her mouth slightly agape for a moment and pulled the corner of her lip between her teeth. "He's not? Maybe he went for a stroll and he's not back from his walk yet."

Major Hunt grabbed a bowl of peas. "Oh, he'll show up sooner or later. I can't imagine him missing a meal."

The remainder of the family followed suit and continued their meal. Brenda was slower than the rest of the family to resume her meal than the others. She showed a great deal of concern on her face.

Mrs. Hunt brought her hand up to her chin and stroked it thoughtfully. "That's odd that he actually is gone for a meal. He has never done that before."

In the Reynolds house, emotions remained tense as Alexander

held his breath. Craig's father carefully and meticulously scanned the forged document and placed it back in Craig's trembling hand. Mr. Reynolds glimpsed at each boy thoughtfully and methodically. He held up a beckoning hand. "Let me see the letter again."

Craig wetted his lips nervously and handed the fake message to his dad.

Mr. Reynolds read the note for what to the boys seemed to be an interminably long time. Craig's father studied each boy's face. "It doesn't seem right that you should leave this soon," he said with a hardened look.

Alexander tried not to stammer and replied, "It's my relatives that found out where I was staying and they are ready for me to come home. I only hope I can reach them in time before they leave on their ship."

Mr. Reynolds stood up and handed the forged paper back to Alexander. "What about the Hunts? Wouldn't they want to see you off?"

"They would, but their car broke down just as we were about to leave. I told them goodbye already. They understand that I am in a hurry."

"Well, I suppose that's true according to the time the ship leaves. Get your stuff in the car. We probably have just enough time to get you there before the ship takes off according to this cable. Let's get going." The boys turned and quickly left the house. Mr. Reynolds followed close behind.

As Craig and Alexander were entering the back seat of the sedan, Mr. Reynolds asked them, "Do you want to say anything to the Hunts before we leave? You could call them on the phone."

"No, that will not be necessary. I am anxious to find my uncle. He will worry about me if I don't get there soon. I don't think it would be right to make him wait."

Craig nudged Alexander in the ribs and beckoned his head towards his father.

Alexander cleared his throat. "Mr. Reynolds, I sure do appreciate you giving me a ride to Anchorage."

"Oh, no problem. Let's just hope we get there before the ship leaves." He put his arm on the top of the car seat and looked back at the boys. "Are you sure it's okay with the Hunts that I give you a ride to see your relatives up there?"

Alexander raised his eyebrows to hide the lie. "Oh sure, I'm just glad that I found out that they are waiting for me up there. Now I won't be a bother to the Hunts anymore. They have enough mouths to feed. My relatives told me they were very anxious for me to come up. Mr. Hunt would have brought me, but like I said, his car is not running. Thanks again."

Mr. Reynolds sighed. "That's okay. I suppose I can check with them later about your phone call when I get back."

Alexander was gaining confidence. "That will be fine. My uncle did tell me that they were leaving tonight for the Soviet Union."

Craig elbowed him in the ribs and whispered so his dad would not hear. "What are you doing?"

Alexander made sure that Mr. Reynolds was not looking and motioned with his hand to Craig that everything would be fine.

Mr. Reynolds made sure that his two young passengers were secure and started the vehicle. The car then whisked off to the north to Anchorage.

Alexander closed his eyes and made a silent earnest wish. *Please let there be a ship there that will take me home to Russia.*

The Hunts were still unaware of Alexander's plan to sneak away until an hour later when Mrs. Reynolds called the Hunts to talk about Alexander. Mrs. Hunt answered the telephone.

"Hello."

"Susan? Hi this is Tina. I just wanted to let you know that I'm sorry to see Alexander leave so soon. He was a nice kid."

Mrs. Hunt stammered. "Leave? Tina, what are you talking about?"

Tina Reynolds slowed her speech. "Alexander is headed to Anchorage with my husband. He was given a cablegram by the boys stating that Alexander's uncle was waiting on a ship for him. He said you could not take him because your car broke down."

Mrs. Hunt gasped. "Oh, my word, Alexander didn't say a thing to us. This is not good. Tina, I'll talk to you later."

She quickly put down the receiver. "Brendan, Brendan!"

The major walked in from the den, frowning at the disruption. "What's up?"

"Brendan, we need to run to Anchorage right away. Alexander lied to the Reynolds, saying that his uncle is on board a ship. He plans to stowaway on a ship."

"When did he leave?"

"I suppose about an hour ago."

Mr. Hunt put his hand on his leg and frowned. "There is no way we can get up there in time. I just hope Greg realizes that Alexander is not supposed to leave and brings him back here. We better wait here and hope for the best. Surely no ship will be leaving this time of the night."

Anchorage Pier # 17 10:00 P.M.

Mr. Reynolds arrived at the pier with the two boys just about the same time that Tina Reynolds had talked to Susan Hunt.

The sun had already set and it was dark except for three street lamps.

Two ships were docked along the pier in the harbor about eighty yards apart. One was a military transport. A small number of American soldiers were coming off.

Mr. Reynolds affirmed his belief that this was the wrong ship. "That's not the ship you're supposed to be on." He continued to drive. "Maybe it's that one." He continued to the far end and parked the car eighty feet away from the ramp of the second ship—a rusty old freighter.

Alexander and Craig jumped out as the car stopped. Craig stuck his head in the car window where his dad was sitting.

Mr. Reynolds was about to exit when Craig pleaded with him. "Dad, could you wait in the car? I want to talk to Alexander alone before he leaves and tell him goodbye. I'll be back in a second."

Mr. Reynolds looked apprehensively around the dock area. "Okay, is Alexander sure he was supposed to meet his uncle here in this area?" The surrounding dock area was dark and foreboding.

Craig nodded. "Yeah, they're supposed to be on that freighter. His uncle works on that ship. It's the one headed to the Soviet Union tomorrow."

Mr. Reynolds wrinkled his nose. "That's surprising considering the war. I didn't think any commercial ships were allowed out into the waters south of here. Maybe it's okay, because the Russians are not in the war yet."

Craig thought quickly. "Oh Dad, you should know that they never shoot at Russian ships. Now you just wait and I'll be right back." He motioned to Alexander. "Come on, the harbor master is over there by that shack. I bet your uncle is there."

Craig and Alexander quickly walked away from the car towards the ship. They walked in a manner that made Mr. Reynolds skeptically lift his right eyebrow.

Alexander rolled his eyes at Craig. "Are you crazy? You shouldn't lie to your father like that."

Craig peered over his shoulder, eyeing his father's car and responded just as quick. "What about you and your supposed 'relatives are in Anchorage' story?"

Alexander spouted back, "It was the only way I could get your father to bring me up here." He swallowed hard, taking in the dank cold sea air. "I hope we get away with this."

Craig looked back at his father in the car. "And what are you going to do when he talks to the Hunts and he finds out that you do not have any family up here? You may be gone, but I'm bound to get a good lickin."

"By the time he calls, I will be well on my way to the Soviet

Union. I'm sorry what is going to happen to you. I'll make it up to you somehow."

Craig whipped his eyes over to the freighter. Rust could be seen running the entire length of the hull. "Are you sure that this ship is guaranteed to head to your country?"

Alexander took in a deep breath. "Somewhere there's bound to be one if I wait long enough. It might even be this ship. I'll be okay."

Craig brought his eyes up somberly. "Well then, take care of yourself." He reached for Alexander's hand. Alexander took it and gave his friend a firm shake. "Good luck."

Alexander smiled. "Thanks."

Craig looked anxiously back towards his father in the car. "By the way, you better make this look good. Act like you are talking to your uncle in the shack. My Dad is watching."

Craig turned and walked slowly to the car. He continued to glance at his Russian friend until he reached the vehicle where his dad had been watching everything with some apprehension.

As Craig turned to the car, he noticed that his father still had a look of doubt on his face. Craig proceeded to get in the vehicle and his dad started the car, but refused to go forward. Mr. Reynolds bent down to look over where Alexander was standing near the shack of the harbormaster. "Will he be okay? This looks like it is a rough neighborhood."

Craig quickly took the initiative. "He should be able find his uncle soon. He'll... he'll be okay."

Mr. Reynolds once again looked over to make sure that Alexander would be okay. He could see the young Russian motioning with his hands as if he were in a conversation with someone. He proceeded to go forward away from the dock, but he still proceeded slowly. "Maybe I should turn around and make sure that he finds his uncle."

Craig bit his lower lip. "There's no need to do that. He is in the main office right now."

Mr. Reynolds frowned, but he continued on. Alexander was now on his own—in a deserted part of Anchorage, in what was probably considered by many to be the worst part of town.

Alexander approached the dark office that was near the offramp of the second ship. He listened as a distant clang of a bell on the military ship shifted through the salty humid air. The sound of the ship's bell added to the feeling of isolation. There was a strong odor of seawater and diesel fuel that permeated the air.

The distant bell chimed once more. Alexander put his hand on his opposite arm and began to wonder if his ruse was such a good idea. His eyes glanced back to where he had left the Reynolds' car. The car was long gone.

Alexander's eyes shifted once more to the old cargo ship. He could see men beginning to fill the deck of the freighter up above him. Apparently they were preparing to come ashore. Alexander believed that it was time to take a chance and ask for assistance. He firmly believed that he would be headed home shortly.

Alexander looked into the gloom of the night and began to second-guess his decision to look for a ship. He wished that the Reynolds' car was still in sight.

Suddenly the stillness of the night was broken. Alexander heard a shout from some rough-looking individuals at the top of the gangplank leading down from the rusty freighter.

Five rough-looking men came stumbling down the ramp. By the manner of their odd behavior and movements, Alexander correctly assumed that they were intoxicated. The rough-looking men stumbled down the ramp, but they were still able to walk, although with some difficulty.

The young Russian decided that this was not a group that he wanted to deal with or trust. He had seen men in Leningrad who had too much to drink and they had a knack to be unpredictable.

Alexander quickly calculated that these were men to be shunned. Alexander turned to leave.

One of the merchant seamen saw Alexander turning to get away. He quickened his stride and ran up to the young Russian with a raised hand trying to slow down the young teenager.

The burly man caught up and put his hand on Alexander's shoulder, who was not expecting such speed out of a drunken sailor. His breath was foul with the stench of a strong whiskey.

The merchant seaman tightened his grip on the young boy. "Hey there now, where are you going?" slightly slurring his words. He brutally forced Alexander around to face him by twisting his shoulders. "Look at me when I am talking to you, friend." He held up a flask. "Why don't you have a drink with us?"

Alexander struggled vainly to get out of the man's grasp. "Please leave me alone."

The other men stumbled forward and surrounded the pair. Alexander knew he was in big trouble. A knot of fear grasped his throat and stomach.

A second sailor heard the Russian's voice. "What kind of accent is that?" he snarled.

The first man put his own hand on his own cheek in mock amazement. "A foreigner. Here we have men fighting overseas and we have the enemy right here."

Another smaller man spun Alexander around by the shoulder. "What are you, a Nazi?" he asked in an accusing manner.

Alexander became belligerent with the very idea of his association with the Nazis. "I am not a German Nazi. I am Russian."

A third man piped in. "The Russians are our enemies too, aren't they?"

The second and smallest seaman quipped, "It doesn't matter." He grabbed Alexander by the shirt. "Well, you're in the wrong place, aren't you, sonny?"

Alexander quivered. "I am trying to get back home." He pointed towards the old freighter. "Does that ship go to Russia?"

The largest man replied with a nasty sneer. "No, it doesn't. We don't go anywhere that has lousy stinking foreigners." He smiled in an evil way and looked at his companions, trying to get their approval. "Hey, I have an idea. This kid is an enemy agent sent here to put a bomb on our ship. Let's send him home in a body bag."

Alexander didn't like what he was hearing, but he had to ask. "What is that—this 'body bag'?"

The short man answered. "It's for dead people. We'll just slit your throat and stuff you in and we'll make sure you get back tò Russia."

That was all Alexander had to hear. In their condition these men would do what they threatened. As they were chuckling at their intimidation antics, Alexander saw his chance. He quickly and deliberately pushed the biggest man and broke out of the encirclement even as they tried to grab him. His best bet for safety was to be around other people. The only ones he saw were men coming off the military transport. Alexander made a beeline for the army transport ship.

The largest merchant seaman tumbled to the ground. He had just been playing around with the teenage boy, but now he was angry.

Rising to his feet, the large man pulled a knife out of a hidden sheath in his sleeve. His friends helped turn him in the right direction. He pushed them aside. With an evil gleam he declared his most foul intentions. "Let's go get him, boys. Let's have a little fun."

The men started scampering after Alexander who was now halfway between the ships. They knew even in their drunken stupor, they would catch the young boy. He looked fast, but they would catch him easily with their longer legs. The man with the knife started to increase his pursuit. "Come back here, Russkie!" he yelled.

Alexander continued to run towards the army transport for all he was worth. He had made the man angry and he could see no other option but to trust the American soldiers coming off the transport.

As he was running, Alexander noticed that the four soldiers coming down the gangplank were black. He had never seen a black person before. In his passing thoughts, Alexander wondered how they would react to him, but he knew that the immediate danger was behind him. He only hoped that he would reach these soldiers before the merchant seamen caught him.

Among the soldiers coming down the ramp was Garrison Kendall. He was a respectable man with a good heart for helping others. He was tall compared to many of the men on the ship, but most of the soldiers that had sailed with him had learned to depend on him. His gentle demeanor was appreciated by both officers and regular enlisted. He would show this in a huge way in short order. He was loyal as a friend and soldier, especially to those in need.

Garrison watched in amazement the action on the flat dock area between the ships. His three friends looked up and wondered what was going on. The man behind Garrison pointed, shifting his rifle higher on his back. "Hey, lookie there. These white boys are chasing each other."

Garrison nodded. "I do believe that young man needs help."

The big-hearted Garrison started running down the gangplank, bringing his rifle off of his shoulder. One of the men behind him called after him. "Oh, let it go. They're not after us."

Garrison ignored his army buddy. He could see that the young boy had a look of terror on his face. Alexander was now approaching the bottom of the gangplank of the military ship, but one of the drunken sailors was right on his tail. It was the man with the knife and he meant to use it. The other merchant seamen were not far behind.

Alexander hit the bottom of the gang plank running.

Garrison was halfway down the plank, trying to make an assessment of the escalating situation.

Alexander, in sheer terror and nearly out of breath, called out to the tall black soldier coming towards him. "Help me. Help me!" Alexander could feel the fear and trepidation pulsing through his body as he ran.

The tallest of the merchant seamen had closed the gap and was nearly breathing down Alexander's neck. The seaman raised his hand to drag Alexander to the ground. Alexander felt the man's grimy hand bounce off his shoulder. The larger adult would soon pull the young man down to the ground where he would be helpless.

Alexander was anxious to get on the other side of Garrison who now stood just ahead on the platform. A collision of the three individuals seemed imminent as a look of terror from Alexander made Garrison brace for a confrontation.

Alexander was nearly out of breath and he called out to the tall black soldier coming towards him. "Please help me!"

CHAPTER 14

The enraged man with the knife advanced closer and closer to the terrified young Russian. The man's face was a contortion of rage and idiocy.

Alexander was fully aware of the seaman's fast panting breath for the man was right behind him. Alexander desperately found some energy and put on a burst of speed and strength. He lunged at the ramp, leaping past Garrison, who had turned sideways so that Alexander could get by him.

"Let them get the little punk," Garrison's shipmates urged as Alexander sped by him, gasping for air as he tried to place bodies between him and his assailants.

Garrison ignored his comrade in arms. The way he saw it, this was a frightened youngster with some very ugly brutes who were meaning to harm him. He could see it in their eyes that they had every intention about harming the boy. He remembered quickly the trust he had as a youngster in someone bigger and wiser when he was in danger. It was time to repay a debt.

As Alexander ran by him, Garrison quickly brought his Garmand rifle off his shoulder and leveled it at the five merchantmen, who as a group, slowed down with the sight of the black soldiers and the fixed rifle posed on Garrison's shoulder.

Garrison calmly ordered, "Hold it right there, boys."

The merchant-seamen abruptly halted at the sight of a rifle pointing at them. Their brains focused a little clearer as the realization of their own possible death was close at hand.

Garrison peered around the sights of his weapon. "Why are you chasing this here youngster?"

Alexander, trying to catch his breath, peered around Garrison's waist.

The first merchant seaman displayed a haughty jaw towards the soldier holding the rifle, although he kept a respectable distance. "Hey spook, watch where you point that thing."

Hearing the word "spook" made Garrison narrow his eyes and he set his right pupil back behind the sight of the rifle, gesturing calmly that he would control the direction of the conversation. "First of all, my name is not 'Spook' and second, you have two seconds to explain yourself. Why are you chasing this here young-un?"

The large merchant seaman sneered at the lone black soldier with a menacing scowl until Garrison snapped the arming bolt action on the rifle.

"Don't make me ask again!" There was a slight nervous pause as Garrison once more narrowed his eyes on the sights of his rifle. "I'll keep pointing this rifle until I get some straight answers."

The three other black soldiers at the top of the ramp advanced in a show of support for their brave friend.

The second merchantman lowered his knife. He pointed at Alexander who was just a few feet behind Garrison, catching his breath, still with a look of apprehension on his young face. "He's a Russkie. I just wanted to prick him a little to see if Russians really do have blue ice water in their veins or see if it's red like mine."

Garrison's eyes focused in an attempt to further discourage the seamen. "What fool notion are you trying to hand me? Leave the boy alone."

The second merchant seaman pointed again with the knife. "He has no business being here in our country. No more than you do."

Without flinching, Garrison puffed out his chest and replied, "This here gun and uniform say I do belong here and even if I didn't have them, I have just as much right as you do to be here."

The smallest of the group of merchant-seamen derided Garrison, "I don't know about that. Why are they sending you boys up here? You might freeze your little fannies off."

Garrison glanced sideways at the men. "I might ask the same of you. Does your skipper know you're on shore and drunk?"

One of the men in the back bluffed his way forward, pointing his finger, "What business is it of yours, darkie?"

Garrison raised his proud chin. "I am an American soldier and as such, I have the right to protect where I see fit, especially for those who need my help."

The largest seaman drew in a breath of the salty laced air trying to summon up his courage. He thumped his fist against his chest. "Well, we don't see it that way."

Seeing that their leader was feeling a little more courageous, the merchantmen advanced as a group, trying to bluff their way past the tall black soldier.

The three black soldiers behind Garrison quickly brought up their weapons to their shoulders and pointed their rifles at the advancing men. The merchant-seamen stopped abruptly in their tracks.

The biggest of the merchantmen muttered, "Stupid darkies. Someone left their brains at home when they issued those boys rifles." Sulking, he motioned with his hand, "Let's get out of here, boys."

With some grumbling, the drunken men began to filter back to the freighter after peering back at the young Russian and the four soldiers with seething eyes.

Garrison looked over his shoulder and grinned at his buddies. "Thanks for not being involved," he remarked sarcastically. He glanced once again in the direction of the retreating merchant-seamen to make sure they would not return. There was no indication that they would come back as they went slinking back to their ship.

The first soldier directly behind Garrison rolled his eyes, trying to avoid his friend's indicting look. "We didn't want them to get you. You owe us too much money." He turned to the men behind him. "Let's get out of here, boys, before this crazy man gets us into any more trouble." He waved at Garrison. "See you later, you crazy fool."

The three men left after making sure that the seamen were gone for good. The night had swallowed up the remnants of the drunken men.

Garrison waved at them as they disappeared into the darkened street. He turned sharply to Alexander. "Are you okay?"

Alexander backed away at the closeness of the big man. "Yeah," he replied as he rubbed his arm. "Thank you."

Garrison gritted his voice. "Boy, what are you doing on the dock anyway? This isn't a safe place for a youngster like you."

Alexander held his head up defiantly. "I was looking for a ship to get back home."

Garrison brought his hand up in an indication of the emptiness of the area. "And what in Heaven's name made you think you would be able to get on a ship this late at night?"

Alexander paused, but spoke out after he noticed he wouldn't get anywhere without an answer. "To Russia."

Garrison raised his eyebrows. "Russia? As long as the Nips are close to the Aleutians, there will be no ship heading to Russia." The man glanced around the dock. There were no vehicles nearby. "How did you get here? I don't see anyone around here!"

Alexander hesitated. "By car."

"Car, what car?" Garrison motioned with his hand. "Come here, boy. Let's find out the entire story."

Alexander hesitated once again, but then he realized that he didn't have much of a choice. He definitely did not want to go back to the freighter. The two young men proceeded to sit down on a nearby curb. Alexander sat down and scooted away from Garrison. Refusing to immediately trust his benefactor, the young Russian tried his best to avoid eye contact with the big soldier.

Garrison rubbed his chin and set his other hand on his rifle that was lying in his lap. "Well, I take it by your accent that you are Russian. How did you get here in Alaska?"

Alexander glanced quickly at the ground. "I can't tell you."

Garrison looked out into the street. "Are you staying with somebody here?"

Alexander wavered and refused to say anything. He tried once more to look anywhere but towards his rescuer. The young boy continued to twist his head to avoid eye contact with Garrison. The Russian thought he had said too much already.

Garrison lowered his voice in a demand. "Well?"

Again there was no answer.

"Boy, you better start talking or I'll leave you alone to face those drunken fools again." Just then a distant bell rang once more. Alexander remembered how it made him feel all alone before and how frightening the dock appeared. The bell, in his mind, indicated the loneliness of the dock.

Alexander bit his lip and pouted, "Those idiots. Why did they do that? Why do they hate me just because I'm a foreigner?"

Garrison softened his tone. "I don't believe it was just you that they hate. Those men were drunk and looking for trouble. I don't think you being a Russian had anything to do with it."

A surprised look over took Alexander's face. "You don't?"

Garrison shook his head. "No, look how they came after me, and I'm just a poor soldier from way down in Alabama."

The young Russian appeared perplexed. "Yeah, how come?"

The soldier replied, "Just plain prejudice, I reckon. It's been going on for ages, but I recollect that those boys don't like much of anything anyway." Garrison held out his hand. "By the way, my name is Garrison... Garrison Kendall."

Alexander scooted closer and took his hand and shook it. "Alexander Baranoff."

Garrison peered at the far ship. "How did you get involved with those men?"

Alexander puckered his lips in remembrance. "I had just arrived on the dock when they were coming off their ship."

Garrison stood up and started down the street. "You know, Alexander, I'm kinda hungry. Come on, why don't you and I get something to eat."

Alexander waited a second and stood up. His hunger pangs were strong, causing him to trust Garrison more. He followed the big black soldier.

The two soon found an all-night greasy spoon café and ordered grilled cheese sandwiches and tomato soup. It wasn't long after that the two began to strike up a conversation, with Garrison leading with questions. His idea was to get Alexander to open up. Garrison was wise in figuring that a good meal would loosen the boy's tongue and he was correct in his assumption. The frightened youngster soon figured out that he was still too young to be striking out on his own in a strange country and he was more than happy to get a hot meal.

Garrison set a napkin on his lap and asked, "So, where are you from in Russia?"

Alexander wiped his mouth to speak, "Leningrad."

"Where were you staying here in Alaska?"

Alexander leaned back. He knew it was no good to hold the truth away from this kind man now. All hope of immediately going back to Russia was for the time being gone. "I… I was staying with a family in Soldotna."

Garrison took a bite of pie. "Well don't you think you ought to get back with them? It's not safe for you to be here alone, not in this neck of the woods anyway."

Alexander's pride was still evident. "Ah, I'll do okay. I can, how do you say, fend for myself."

Garrison raised his eyebrows. "Like you did with those goons." He casually picked up a sourdough dinner roll. "Alexander, I want to tell you something. You and I are in the same boat."

"How's that?"

"We're both a long ways from home, and we both have hurts. I live in a far-away city called Huntsville and believe me, I get mighty lonesome for those hotcakes of my mother's loving hands."

Alexander looked down, remembering his own mother and her meals.

Garrison continued, "I know you can't get back to Russia now, but there's a family in Soldotna that is probably just as good to you. Why don't you go back to them?"

Alexander twisted his bottom lip. "I don't know how. I lied to these people to get a ride up here."

The big soldier straightened up his back and reached into his front pocket. "I have some change. Let's give them a call. I bet they're wondering where you are right now."

Alexander paused and finally nodded his head. Together, the young black soldier and the Russian boy scooted out of the booth of the diner and headed to the pay telephone.

Soldotna

The young Russian regretted deeply how he had worried everyone, but the Hunts understood his desire to go home.

To his amazement, Alexander was forgiven for his unwise action. The only reprimand that he received was being reminded how worried everyone in the Hunt family had been during his absence. Alexander still wanted to go back to the Soviet Union, but he decided that the timing was not right for such an endeavor.

In the beginning, Alexander's time in America passed slowly, due to his painful memories of the past. His adjustment to the United States territory was hard, but soon his mood depended on what events happen with the Hunt family.

The following year was both a time of happiness and sadness for the Hunt family. Major Hunt was called away for active duty. Part of his duty was supervising soldiers on the construction of the huge project in Canada called the Alaskan Highway, now being built in case the Japanese invaded Alaska.

Later that year the major was sent to a small Pacific island that was one of the first of lost territory to be invaded by the Americans. The island was called Guadalcanal. The war brought the real possibility to the Hunt family that he could be killed in action.

The family knew it would be hard to live a normal life without the major. No one could replace him at home, but Alexander filled in wherever possible. Technically, he was the man of the house until the major returned. Mrs. Hunt was grateful for the upkeep of the house by the Russian lad and he did his job well.

Perhaps the happiest member of the house of Alexander's decision to stay a little longer, was Brenda, although she tried hard not to show it.

As Alexander became more acquainted with the some of the other young people of Soldotna, two of his classmates became good friends with him.

Craig Reynolds, the boy who had tried to help Alexander at Anchorage and received a mild punishment in the form of a stern speech, grew to like the young man from Russia more and more with each passing day. He didn't hold Alexander responsible for getting into trouble when they had lied about the ship.

Another young man that befriended Alexander was Paul Grayson. Paul was younger than Craig or Alexander, but he was taller than either one of his friends. Paul's two main interests were football and wrestling. At times he would be taken advantage of by the young ladies of the town because, like Harrison, he considered himself to be a ladies' man.

This trio of young men was soon seen everyday roaming the streets of Soldotna like good buddies. Most of this camaraderie came about because they had a common bond. They all had a person that hated them. It was the local high school bully, Harrison Fisher.

Harrison Fisher had few friends inside the school. No matter the situation, Harrison expected everything to go his way. If it didn't work for him, he would try just about anything to make a change for his ultimate benefit.

Seeing the popularity of Alexander, Craig and Paul grow, Harrison was determined to intimidate these three classmates into submission and make them buckle to his authority. It would be a lifelong animosity.

Another person who decided from the start that he didn't like Alexander was Thomas McClary, a self-made bully with less of a mean streak than his buddy, Harrison Fisher, but he had a reputation for a nasty disposition just as well.

Thomas, who was fairly new to Alaska, was a hard-headed individual whose father grew up in the rougher part of San Francisco. He had transferred much of his lifestyle to his son and always expected him to be tough.

After hearing about the job boom in Alaska, Thomas' father brought his family to Soldotna. The reputation of staying tough stuck with Thomas even though he was among a different breed of people—folks who tried at first to be nice to the young man.

After being spurned so many times, many residents saw Thomas as a trouble-maker and the reputation seemed to follow him to the letter. Many bruised and battered children had their encounter with him and now he was especially unkind to one young man, a young Russian by the name of Alexander.

The two fifteen-year-old boys, Harrison and Thomas, were drawn together as their personalities dictated. It would be a life-long common hatred of the do-gooders of the school and of the good virtues in the village. Thus two opposing factions were forming in the little town of Soldotna. They would all grow up with the boy from the Soviet Union, but this was to be the extent of their common traits. Political and historical events would bring a course that would often bring on a clash of ideologies and emotions.

It would be a struggle that even the town would endure as townspeople took sides in the conflict. Some, because of their distrust and outside fear of foreigners; others because of their hate of bullies.

Over the next two years, Alexander would grow quite fond of his adopted family. They had shared with him the average life of an American citizen and Alexander liked what he saw. With this new influx of culture and lifestyle, Alexander began to understand what it was like to act and feel as an American. His resolve to return to the Soviet Union was weakening every day that he spent with his foster family. The Hunts had inserted a great deal of influence on him and much of it was how they had treated him, just like one of the family. This type of caring was especially true with Brenda and how she related to the young man. At first it was brotherly love, but soon it would turn into something more.

During his stay, Alexander found himself being drawn slowly to the older girl, Brenda Hunt. In the days that he spent with the Hunts, Alexander and Brenda became fast friends. He liked the way she could relate to others so well and her charms were as gracious as her mother's.

Brenda discovered too that she was quickly being drawn to the young Russian. He was tall and handsome and he was unlike any conception that she had of the Russian people. The young Russian was smitten by the American girl's charms. Alexander spent many long hours with Brenda, finding out more about the United States and how the country operated. Alexander was curious about her politics, her economics, and her customs. The more the young Russian heard, the more he liked. The fact that he wanted to spend time with Brenda was a great factor as well. As much as he had loved his family, Alexander was slowly learning to dislike his country, even though the words of his father still echoed in his ears: "Don't become involved with Americans."

"What was the main reason that you are having doubts about the Soviet Union?" Brenda asked bluntly one day. She had her suspicions that Alexander was struggling with his early teachings.

"I remember the rumors before the war about the Premier. Stalin was a man full of mystery and dark secrets. Many people disappeared during the time of peace. Many of these people vanished on the orders of Stalin. People do not disappear suddenly in your country. It is unlike that in Russia. You are allowed to say many things without getting into trouble. I know now that Stalin is a cruel and hateful dictator. His mentality was almost as bad as Hitler's. I lost many friends and relatives simply because they criticized the Soviet system. I never saw them again. I know that some died in the labor camps of Siberia." Alexander looked up at Brenda with a somewhat sad smile. "I wonder if I go back, maybe I would disappear one day. I can't trust my feelings and they would betray me. I have seen the freedom that you as Americans have and I would take back with me what I have seen and heard."

Brenda had a solution. "Alexander, you need to learn more about your own country and ours. That way you can make your own comparisons."

"But what if I make the wrong choice?"

Brenda smiled sweetly. "Then leave all you can that is bad and then you won't go wrong."

He beamed a large grin at her. "I'll do that."

As the days went by and the war continued, Alexander's stay presented complications for the young Russian. Deep down in his heart, Alexander was definitely convinced that he did not want to return to the Soviet Union, but there was a part of him that wanted to honor the memory of his father. In part, he was afraid of what might happen to him on his return because of his pro-American stance, but in a larger sense he trusted his instincts about the American people he had met and he had become anxious lately to learn more. There was a spirit about these people that welcomed the young man into their society. For the most part, Americans were very nice and he wanted to stick around to see if it would last. Slowly he came to the conclusion that his father had been wrong about these people, and they just didn't care about money like his father had taught him.

The boy adjusted quickly to his new life, once he got over the fact that he would never see his parents again. His loneliness for them faded eventually because the void had been filled.

In the meantime, Alexander was learning much about American democracy from his adopted family whom he was gradually learning to love. They had taken him into their hearts and he responded in kind. Along with their compassion he was also learning much about Alaska with its rich history and natural resources, particularly the fishing industry. The salmon were abundant and workers were needed to harvest the fish. Alexander saw this as an opportunity for future work.

One more item Alexander added to his edification was the unintentional lesson of infatuation. It would hit him like a whirlwind.

One particular afternoon, Brenda approached the young Russian as he sat outside the house, intent on asking many direct questions.

Each question that Brenda directed at the young Russian was intent on annoying him. Brenda renewed her outspokenness about the faults of the Soviet Union. Her real intention was to tease Alexander to the point where she could take advantage of him. "You never did tell me what it is like where you are from. Can you talk about it now? Is Russia all what it is cracked up to be?"

Alexander blinked at her in confusion.

Brenda had caught him off guard, so she continued, "I mean, is it all that great?"

"It is the most wonderful place in the world," came the hesitant reply.

"It can't be all that great. I heard the people are fat and ugly."

"That is a lie. The Russian people are quite beautiful."

"Even their women? Who do you think is better looking, the Russian girls or the American girls?"

Alexander was wary. This was a dangerous question.

"Alexander, I asked you a question. Are American girls pretty?" Brenda was nervous, but she wanted a commitment. She knew Alexander wouldn't bring up the subject. She would force the issue now. "Well?" She gazed intently at him determined to get an answer.

Chapter 15

The young man's face purposely took on a blank stare. Alexander, accomplishing in his mind a mischievous nature, decided to irritate his obnoxious friend. He had no desire to satisfy his surly antagonist with the truth.

Without hesitation the young man shrugged his shoulders and crinkled his mouth with a crooked and slight grin. "American girls are okay, but the cold winds of my country produce the most beautiful women in the world. Even the plainest of Russian girls would out-dazzle and outshine even the prettiest of American girls, and that includes insolent Alaskan girls." His defiant smile deepened to agitate Brenda even more.

Brenda puckered her lips in disgust and pouted. "Oh, what do you know? I heard Russian boys are not particularly bright either." Her eyes narrowed as she glared at the young Russian. Alexander maintained his silly grin.

Brenda was incensed. She tossed her long brown hair over her shoulder and placed her clenched hands angrily on her hips. "Alexander, you are a rude and arrogant young scalawag. You know what? I will have no trouble at all saying 'Goodbye!' to you when you go back to your own country, and it can't be soon enough for me. The very nerve of suggesting that Russian girls are more beautiful." The young lady tighten the gaze of her beautiful dark brown eyes and brought her hands up as if ready to pounce on Alexander. "I should tell you that Alaskan men are far more intelligent and handsome than Russian rogues."

With that belligerent statement, Brenda turned and went back into the house in an indignant posture.

Alexander smiled slightly in triumph. He rather liked getting under the skin of this considerably pretty girl that had constantly antagonized him in the past. In his opinion, he was finally able to get back at the impertinent American girl, who up to now had been able to get the best of him with all her nasty verbal jabs.

Now that Brenda was gone, he looked around the yard for other possibilities for a fun activity. Nothing stood out as being motivating. "Oh well," he muttered. "I can think of other things to do that are just as fun." He briefly thought of going into town to find Craig and Paul. Possibly the three of them could find something to do.

Alexander turned his head to face the town. He sought a new activity. He looked back into the house and thought briefly about annoying Brenda again. "No, I better not." He didn't wish to throw too many insults at Brenda. He eventually wanted her as a friend, not a lifetime enemy.

Alexander was about to run on down to the fishing dock, when noticed a delicious aroma coming from the direction of the house. Through the open kitchen window, Alexander could see Mrs. Hunt setting some type of pastry on a multi-colored hot pad to cool. Mrs. Hunt was trying out a new recipe for apple strudel.

"American women can cook," he verified in his mind. The smell of the strudel had an over-powering affect on the young man. Alexander could not resist most of Mrs. Hunt's recipes. He slowly was drawn by the scent into the kitchen.

Mrs. Hunt glanced over as the young teenager came strolling in. "Are you ready for some strudel?" she asked in her usual gentle manner.

"Yes ma'am!" The boy obediently sat down at the table.

"It won't be long. The strudel needs to set for a while." Mrs. Hunt began to hum a tune. Alexander recognized it as a Christian hymn.

Oh boy, Alexander thought to himself. *Here she goes again. If I want a piece of strudel, I need to stay put and listen to her ranting about her silly belief of God.* The boy was befuddled, but yet curious. One aspect about the Hunt family that Alexander was having trouble relating to was the importance religious activity seemed to play in their lives. Alexander, with his strong communist indoctrination, could not comprehend how an entire family could be taken in by something that in his mind didn't exist.

In his long walks with Brenda Hunt, Alexander would ask many questions about the weekly ritual that took place on Sundays of going to church. If Brenda's answers seemed insufficient, the young man was just interested enough to ask his hostess in seeking the insufficient answers.

Brenda's mother was more than happy to answer each question that Alexander would bring to her. Today was no different. He looked up from his thoughtful, but serious gaze. "Mrs. Hunt, why is church so important to Americans?"

"Well not all Americans believe in going to church. There are many who have no interest in it at all."

Alexander ravenously gazed at the strudel. "They must be the smart ones. They are the people that can't be swayed by fables and myths. Mrs. Hunt, how is it that you can believe in a being that you can't see or feel? We Russians were taught to believe that nothing is real unless you can actually prove that it is a fact. Isn't it the Americans that are always saying, 'Seeing is believing'?"

"Alexander, I understand that your parents had no feelings for you." Brenda's mother knew she was taking a chance to make such a statement.

Alexander's facial features indicated intense anger and shock. He could not believe that Mrs. Hunt would make such a statement. "Who told you such a ridiculous lie?"

"You just did."

"Huh?"

Mrs. Hunt displayed the sweet smile that seemed to be prevalent in her family. "You just told me that there is no such thing that cannot be seen without research to prove that it is real. Love is an unproved myth because you cannot see it. Your parents could not have possibly have loved you according to what you have just told me."

Alexander's face quickly took on an air of indifference and smugness. "There is a great difference between love and a make believe person in Heaven. How do you know of his existence?"

"How do you know that your parents actually loved you? Not everything we know about can be seen physically. Feelings and emotions are part of our world, but how do we know they exist?"

Alexander shrugged his shoulders. He liked Mrs. Hunt too much to argue.

Mrs. Hunt grabbed a spatula for the strudel. "I'll tell you the answer. There is something that is inside all of us that yearns for compassion and love. When it is filled, we know very well it took something real to fill it. It's no different with spiritual qualities and attributes. I know that there is a God for he fills an empty place in my heart." She put her gentle hand upon his shoulder. "I feel his tenderness and compassion and I know he lives there. To tell the truth, this was probably not an easy task for him either. I believed like you that God was just something that somebody made up a long time ago. You will have to experience God first to know that he is real. The time came when I began to believe and eventually I was convinced that there is a loving and kind spirit out there that I could reject or accept." Mrs. Hunt smiled softly at her charge. "I accepted."

She turned towards her ward. "Alexander, I know in times of great trials, I can always turn to him. You might say I turn my problems into prayers. I'm not saying that I don't have problems, but believing in Jesus, I can find the good in life and focus on it."

Alexander squirmed. He was increasingly becoming uncomfortable because of the direction of the conversation. "I think I will go find out what Brenda is doing." He quickly stood up and started for the door.

"Didn't you want some strudel?" Mrs. Hunt called out when she could see she was losing a customer. It was hard to believe that someone would walk out on her cooking.

Alexander paused briefly, but decided the tasty treat was not worth the conversation. He started for the door again.

"Alexander, remember this: you are free to choose what path you take. Destiny is only a small part of our future." Alexander quickened his pace. Mrs. Hunt noticed the acceleration and called out. "If you ever need more information on the subject, just let me know, and if at all possible, maybe someday you would like to go to a church service with us and find out some more?"

"No thanks." Alexander quickened his pace. "I think I have all the answers I need."

Alexander left her presence a little stunned on what had just been discussed, but it made him think long and hard.

Mrs. Hunt knew what to say to Alexander to make him comprehend the reality of another life. She was an expert with young minds and she had worked her expertise with the young Russian.

Alexander didn't mind all that much to learn from Mrs. Hunt, but he felt compelled to learn more from Brenda. Perhaps her answers could be combated with good communist doctrine.

Alexander stopped briefly in his tracks. He wasn't sure if Brenda would talk to him after the way he had teased her, but he decided the risk was worth it and set out again to seek her company.

Why it was true that Brenda had overcome her temporary anger and was willing to talk to the young Russian in earnest dialogue, she was not willing to let this rude young man off with easy answers. Brenda was just as determined as her mother and made it her personal duty to make Alexander think hard about the afterlife and his existence in general.

Alexander quickly located Brenda sitting outside on a curb. Alexander sat beside her. "Your mother, she's at it again."

"What are you talking about?" Brenda inquired as she scooted over to make room for the young man.

"Oh, your mother is talking about religion and how it would do me some good. If there is something I can't stand it is being told that I need some preaching. She knows that I can't believe in God. Why does she do that?"

Brenda leaned over as if to tell a secret. "Do you want the truth?"

Alexander nodded his head in a halfway non-communicative response.

"Why don't we go up on the hill where the large spruce tree is located? We can talk about it there."

"What if I don't want to go?"

"Oh, come on and keep me company." Brenda stood up and held out her hand.

Alexander couldn't resist the gesture. Brenda's eyes glistened as she coaxed him on. It was very hard to resist her persuasive and soft brown eyes. "Well, if it will give me a break from your mom's heavy dose of religious ideology, I suppose I'll come with you."

The two teenagers walked steadily to the large Sitka blue-green spruce that grew on the hillside overlooking Soldotna and the Cook Inlet. Behind them laid a forest grove of serene deep green foliage. The soft scent of moisture filled the air with wild flowers as the breeze swept in from the surrounding hills.

Brenda laid flat on her stomach below the large Sitka spruce tree facing down the hill in a prone position facing away from her house. The view she faced was set towards the large Cook Inlet just beyond the house. She gracefully sniffed a forget-me-not lying between her elbows.

Alexander preferred to sit up with his back against the tree so he could view the fishing fleet of the town. A small gull flew over the pair, screeching at the two humans trying to coax them into throwing up a morsel of food. The salty air was fresh with the soft scent of the briny deep and an invigorating spruce fragrance.

Alexander gazed out over the beauty and peacefulness of the surrounding area and yet he was troubled. "I cannot understand all of this," he suddenly exclaimed out to his friend lying on the grass. "How can one place be so peaceful, while somewhere on the same planet it can be so violent?"

Brenda tried to use her words of encouragement, "We don't always have the choice of where we live, but we usually have a choice to go somewhere else during our life."

Alexander frowned, "I guess that is true, but can such a peace be held on to forever in one place? Will mankind ever find complete joy and satisfaction somewhere on this earth?"

Brenda turned her eyes downcast. "I have known a lot of people who claim that they are quite content with life. The world is not perfect, but I know that these people can usually cope with any situation. My mother is such a person, bless her heart." She returned her eyes to Alexander. "I know I have been quite happy since you have come to Alaska."

Alexander blushed. He wasn't quite ready for a compliment from the girl that he enjoyed teasing so much. His face turned serious once again. "That's another thing I don't understand. How can you believe in such happiness when you believe in things that can't possibly exist?"

Brenda was about to frown at the remark, but then she hit upon an insight on how to reply. "Maybe my happiness was based on something that is real. I know there is someone deep down in my heart that cares for me. I know he exists."

Alexander scoffed at her suggestion. "It is all based on emotions. Where is the scientific proof of God's existence?"

"Where is the scientific proof of love and a visual proof of the wind? There is no earthly reason for it, but do the beings of this planet make sense half the time? Look at your homeland. Humans don't always have all the answers and they keep making mistakes, even with all their scientific agendas and theories. Isn't it reasonable to assume that there are other factors that control our lives? There could be other beings that we can't even imagine about in our minds, beings that do exist even if we can't see them. What about angels, God, Satan? Could they be legends or facts that most men cannot accept? I happen to believe that they do exist. It is an unscientific theory or fact that is called faith."

Brenda paused briefly from her soapbox speech. She motioned with her eyes for Alexander to look out towards the Cook Inlet. "Look at everything our God has created and provided for mankind. Everything, including this big, wondrous planet is according to God's wondrous plan. Think of the type of a beautiful place this would be if we knew how to treat it right."

Alexander was ready with a preconceived answer. "What about death and war and famine?"

"For the most part all these catastrophes were created by man, not God. We know that man is not perfect and he has a free will to do whatever he wants, even to create death and disease for others. You have to remember as well that there is another force out there that is responsible for creating the type of chaos that we are now experiencing. Man can even be influenced by his own treachery."

"Satan is another figment of man's imagination. I can't believe in such nonsense."

Alexander frowned at Brenda's attempt to persuade him into believing about God and Satan. Brenda felt frustrated as well and pouted silently for a moment, believing that she was getting nowhere with Alexander.

Alexander bristled. "Why would a God of love allow a scoundrel like Adolph Hitler to exist?"

"God loves every man, even Hitler, but he hates his sin and the sins of everyone else. Hitler was responsible for his type of life, not God!" Brenda decided to change her tactics. "Let me ask you something," Brenda said smiling. "Would you ever consider being one of Hitler's puppets?

"Absolutely not!"

"That's what I thought. Well, believe me, that is exactly what he wants, for you to be his slave and puppet. God, on the other hand, does not want man to be a puppet. God created the world so that man could show his love freely, without being forced into it."

"It is hard to accept such things without proof."

Brenda smiled. She now knew that Alexander was thinking hard about spiritual matters. "Alexander, you are going to do whatever you want to do, but just maybe your life has a direction that you thought never would exist. Now is your chance to change. I want you to know that change is always hard, but sometimes it has to happen. It was already set into motion. Think about it."

Brenda stood up. "I'll see you back at the house." She paused and watched him for a second as he looked at the ground, contemplating the mass of thoughts whirling through his brain.

Brenda left Alexander to overlook the bay. Alexander watched the blazing gold and crimson sunset and chewed on a bit of grass. He leaned his fist against his temple.

"I must think seriously about my future and where it is taking me," he thought as he watched the setting sun. "If I never find the answers now, I may never find out." The young Russian slowly tilted his eyes towards the heavens in a puzzled look of despair, maybe seeking an answer in the sky above. "What am I that I need to be treated this way? It only adds to my loneliness and confusion. Where are all the answers?"

Only the sea breeze responded to his whispers of anguish. Alexander paused to hang his head, wondering. His mind whirled with the thoughts of the past, primarily with what had happened during the attack on Dutch Harbor. "Why did it have to be that my parents had to be brutally murdered? What about little Treleska back in Leningrad? Why take their lives and not mine?"

In the silhouette of the brilliant red Pacific sunset, Alexander began shedding tears. He again lowered his head in unreserved sense of shame in the midst of the beautiful setting array of brilliance. Alexander rotated his head towards his homeland in the west. He could only think of the solidarity of his heart and could feel the unwanted encroachment of self-pity where he believed that no one else could share what he was going through.

Alexander heard the screech of a seagull and he peered up, reacting to the sound as a single bird flew straight at him and he ducked. The gull was accustomed to flying towards the humans to entice them to throw food up to it. Alexander could only envision in his mind a Zero heading towards his father and cutting him down with a salvo of bullets. His momentary delusion was cleared up as he picked up his step and headed back to the Hunt house. As he came nearer to the house, Alexander could see Brenda watching him in bewilderment. She could sense that the young Russian was having doubts about life.

Alexander regained his composure as his interest focused on the seagull that had followed him. The bright pink and orange rays of the sun sparkled in near perfect reflection on the calm waters of the ocean. The serenity of the scene upon the glassy seawater calmed his spirit.

Alexander raised his head in response to the soft wind blowing into his nostrils where a gentle fragrance of the nearby alpine forest enhanced his senses. The combined sea breeze and spruce forest scent invigorated his mind. "Russia was never like this!" He smiled. "Everywhere I've been it seems that all countries have their own scent. Some are better than others. Maybe I can adjust to another world other than my own." He peered back at Brenda, who was halfway home. "At least I have a friend here, a very good friend."

He slowly walked down the path to the Hunt household. When he walked through the door, Mrs. Hunt was waiting for him in the living room. She handed him a letter. The postmark stated that the letter was from Alabama.

Chapter 16

"Who would write me from Alabama?" Alexander wondered. "I know that Garrison lived there, but he is still fighting somewhere in the South Pacific as far as I know." He scanned the heading on the front of the envelope. Alexander did not immediately recognize the sender. It was from a Mrs. Wynona Charles from Huntsville. Alexander could not understand why this woman who he had never met before would write him. Curious, Alexander opened the letter with some trepidation.

Alexander read part of the letter and faltered in his stance. He brought the letter down to his side.

Mrs. Hunt was concerned. "Is it bad news?"

Alexander's face was a mask of agony. He handed the letter to Mrs. Hunt.

It was from Garrison Kendall's sister, the man who had saved him from the drunken merchant sailors.

Mrs. Hunt briefly read the letter to herself and looked up to Alexander, gently placing a caring arm around his shoulders. The rest of the family was unsure what to do. Mrs. Hunt could see that they wanted more information. Softly she uttered, "May I share this with the family?"

Alexander nodded slowly. Mrs. Hunt started from the beginning.

Dear Alexander,

It is with great sadness that I send you this letter. My brother spoke about you often and I'm sure he would want you to know what had happened to him. Garrison was mortally wounded on Guadalcanal this past month. With what I have heard from his army buddies, he died as bravely as any man could.

You are probably wondering how I was able to get the information to write to you about his demise. His letters to us spoke many times of the young Russian boy that gave him hope and courage. He told us several times how during his duty in Alaska about meeting with this certain young boy who really needed a friend at a most difficult time and how my brother was there to help. Through this he told us how hope in you made him a better person because he felt good about himself in helping you. I regret to say that his beautiful life has now come to an end. Life can be so beautiful, he would often tell me, but it was especially nice when he had the joy to have you for a friend. He saw in you a goodness that did not exist in a lot people that he had been associated with during his all too brief life. His friendship with you and your great kindness constantly inspired him to see everyone in a Christian light.

I just wanted to say, thank you for being a part of his life. He remembered you well through all your correspondence with him. He had often mentioned in his letters that if anything were to happen to him that one of his last requests was to wish you the best. Your letters were a great comfort for him and again I thank you for that. He enjoyed them immensely in his times of loneliness. Thank you for being his friend.

Sincerely, Wynona

Alexander choked back tears as he gently took the letter back. The letter quivered in his hands. He had just sent a letter to the man who had saved his life. It would soon come back unopened. In it, Alexander was going to tell Garrison how life was becoming easier to tolerate and how it was becoming more precious to him every day.

Alexander had learned patience from Garrison and now he was gone. The young man couldn't help but feel a little cynical about life at that moment. He decided to retire to the outdoors to be alone with his thoughts. A very good friend, Garrison Kendall, had died on Guadalcanal and it was time to mourn. It was yet another setback in the life of Alexander Baranoff.

Inside the house, not a word was spoken. Brenda implored an approving look from her mother to go after the young Russian and console him. Her mother, understanding what was going on in her daughter's mind, for once did not know whether it would be wise to let her go after him. She wanted to respect the young man's privacy, but knew that he should share his grief with someone who was close to him. She nodded a slight approval to Brenda.

In her own mind, Brenda wondered if she would be intruding into an area of the boy's life that he would deem as unwelcome. She hesitated briefly and thought about her options, considering Alexander's feelings and the possible outcome of her intrusion. He might resent her for the rest of his stay in America. Yet she reasoned that he really wanted to share his feelings with someone at this difficult time. He really needed to be given a chance for consoling. She followed the young man up the hill.

Alexander was sitting in a glade on top of a large granite boulder. Brenda stopped and she advanced slowly.

Alexander sensed her presence, but did not turn his face towards her. He continued to sadly stare at the interior of the forest with a slight breeze blowing wisps of his hair sideways.

As Brenda came within an arm's length of the boy, Alexander blurted out, "It's not fair. No one should endure what I have gone through." Tears were coursing down his cheeks. He continued to look deep into the nearby fir trees.

Brenda walked into his line of view. "Alexander, I know there is nothing I can do to change what has already happened, but I'm here if you need someone to talk to."

Alexander didn't smile at the gesture, but the corners of his mouth came up slightly. He choked out the words, "I'll be okay."

Brenda turned to go back home, but Alexander held her up as he softly grabbed her arm. "Can you help me make it through this?"

"Of course," she said softly as she put her caring arms around his neck.

Alexander responded as he wrapped his arms around her waist and laid his cheek on her abdomen. He closed his eyes, trying to drive out the sorrow and grief that had invaded his heart and soul.

The embrace lasted only a couple of minutes, but it signified, at least for now, a strong bond of mutual friendship between the boy from Russia and the girl from Alaska.

March 17, 1943

Spring always came late to the Alaskan mainland, but yet there was something extraordinary about the manner in which the season had come to the countryside. The people of the land were viewing life in many different and sometimes bewildering ways.

Perhaps because of the war, people were more aware of their surroundings along with the people that were different and new. Even growing up took a new form and young people grew up in a different world. Maturity became more commonplace in the young people of Alaska, and in some cases a necessity. Fathers had died in the war and mass responsibility was suddenly thrust upon young boys. With the possibility of any new disaster, children understood all too well that they might have to go from the mindset of a child to the responsibility of an adult at anytime.

The season of spring brought this to light with the young Russian as well. He had seen his own father die and he had enough respect for the Hunt family that he realized that he might be called to take care of them too.

Alexander's feelings for each member of the family were changing and during this particular year, Alexander and Brenda could no longer see each other as childhood companions that had at one time played immature games. Feelings were growing stronger with advance adolescence and each young teenager was gradually seeing the traits that were inherited in the opposite sex. Their differences were more notable and their behavior was adjusted accordingly. Even their conversations were more dignified in trying to hide their childish past.

In one way, Alexander treated Brenda like a younger sister, but this was primarily for show. Their true feelings for one another were growing stronger with each passing day, but they hid them well from each other. It was another difficulty that Alexander had to face, even though he could tolerate this endeavor for the time being.

Another major change was in the way in which Alexander now accepted more responsibility for his living quarters. He no longer felt that he could live off the Hunts without paying back their hospitality. He took his duty seriously and thought it was time to earn his keep.

Alexander soon found out that workers were needed for the local fishing fleet and with the summer approaching, Alexander signed on with one of the boats. It became routine for the boats to go out early and come back fairly late in the afternoon. Alexander learned to love the great outdoors through these trips.

As the fishing increased into spring and summer, the days became longer. The fishing boat skippers wanted to increase their haul of fish so they could reap the rewards of financial gain. As the summer progressed, they stayed out on the waters of Alaska longer and longer. There were many nights that Alexander came home exhausted because of the extra work, but he enjoyed the challenge and was diligent in what he did for a living.

June 7, 1943

It was late one particular cool night when Alexander came in after a long haul out at sea. He was anxious for sleep and food. Alexander was bone weary tired and he was glad to come in from another long day. He was hungry and was looking forward to the cooking of Mrs. Hunt. The boat chugged slowly into the docking area and Alexander noticed a familiar figure waiting for him.

Even in the evening dusk, Brenda's radiant face showed the light of her happiness. Alexander could feel a little pride for everyone on board the boat knew that Brenda was there only for one person. Alexander jumped off the boat tied up the docking vessel. Brenda had waited for him and wanted to talk to him. He glanced up at her and walked right by to where she was standing. Her constant chatter about America was starting to make sense and it bothered him. He almost wanted to avoid her.

Without so much as a faint hello, he skirted around her and proceeded to walk up the hill, trying to ignore her.

Brenda followed him at a distance. She quickened her pace and caught up with him just before they reached the house. They were both about to sit down in the living room when Christopher, one of the youngest boys, suddenly burst into the same room where Brenda and Alexander were thinking about continuing their conversation.

Christopher held up the recent edition of the newspaper in triumph. "Look here, Alexander, look here!" he said in a high-pitched voice. "The Japanese have been cleared off Attu and Kiska in the west. They no longer control the Bering Strait. Alexander, do you know what this means?" He said with exuberance. "You will be able to go back home pretty soon!"

"Yeah, that's just great," Alexander mumbled with clenched teeth. His eyes shifted to Brenda to catch her reaction.

Christopher looked at Alexander with a puzzled look. He couldn't understand why Alexander didn't react in the same excitement that he had.

Brenda looked at her friend with solemn eyes. She could tell that Alexander was struggling with the situation. She hoped deep down that he would decide to stay.

"Here let me see that!" Alexander gently grabbed the paper and opened it up. His eyes shifted upwards to each member of the Hunt family. Everyone stood quietly trying see what Alexander's reaction would be. Alexander shifted his eyes over to Brenda and to each of the Hunt family members and said, "Christopher is right. The American army has beaten the Japanese in the Aleutians. I guess there is nothing to prevent me from going home now."

Mrs. Hunt heard the commotion and walked into the room. She gave an appearance of a forced half-smile. She had heard the conversation from the other room and waited for Alexander's reaction. She glanced at Brenda, knowing precisely how she would respond.

Alexander gradually nodded. He silently laid the paper down slowly on the table. Suddenly he stopped himself in mid-stride. His heart spoke volumes to where his life would take him. He admitted deep inside to himself that being in Alaska had been a great experience. He had to get it out. With a serious face Alexander decided to proclaim what his possible near future would be.

Before Alexander could say anything, Major Hunt, home on leave, stood up from the corner lounging chair where he had been sitting quietly. He cleared his throat. "We'll miss you, son. I'll call the State department and see what arrangements can be made to get you home."

Brenda swallowed hard. She wasn't ready to hear about Alexander's departure. She could feel her stomach churning. Her face was beset with wavering tightness and she knew that if the resolve to keep a straight face didn't work, she knew full well that the tears could come at any time. Her true and loyal companion for the last three years would be going back home to Russia soon. She had known all along that it was a strong possibility that she would never see Alexander again. Tears seeped into her eyes. Faking a cough, she ran outside to be alone. She didn't want the handsome young man to leave, especially this soon. Her deepest thoughts confirmed that Alexander Baranoff had become her very best friend.

CHAPTER 17

Alexander scanned the floor in profound thought. Something deep inside of the young man was telling him that going to Russia now would be terribly wrong. He brought his chin up and looked Major Hunt directly in the eyes. "Just because the Japanese are out of the Aleutians does not change the situation all that much. There is still a war going on and I feel that I would be much safer here than I would be at home. The Germans are still a considerable threat to my homeland. If you don't mind my company a little bit longer, I would like to stick around here for the time being, if that is okay with you?" With that proclamation, Alexander waited for a response.

Major Hunt smirked as he glanced towards the other members of his family who simultaneously beamed broadly their approval. "I think that would be fine with all of us." He put a reassuring hand on Alexander's shoulder. "Alexander, if it's your desire to stay here you are more than welcome and honestly that would be all right with me."

Alexander smiled. "I'd like that very much." His eyes shifted to find Brenda and he surmised that she had slipped outside. He decided to find her and share his news.

Alexander went out where Brenda was sitting on the steps of the porch. She tried to avoid his eyes for she knew he would see it as an act of caring, which she didn't want to reveal to him. It would be a sign of weakness in her mind.

Finally as he approached her, Brenda managed to look up at him.

Alexander sat down beside her. He delayed his intended implication to her, but finally and delicately declared, "I'm not leaving, Brenda."

Brenda stood up. "Really!" Then she softened her voice trying to hide her jubilation. "Oh, really?"

Alexander smiled slightly. He could see that Brenda was ecstatic even though she did her best not to show it. She grinned brightly at Alexander and tossed her head upwards in a small gesture of defiance. She didn't want to give Alexander the impression that she cared. *I won't give him the satisfaction of knowing that I like him. After all, he has been so rude to me in the past,* she thought.

She looked at him with an air of indifference.

Alexander scrunched up his nose in confusion. *The little snob, what does she have to be so rude about?* he thought. *Oh well, I'll just do the best I can to get along with her.* He turned to face Brenda. "All things considered, I thought you would be interested."

"Umm, yeah, thanks for letting me know," she said nonchalantly. She turned and went inside the house. Once inside she clenched her fist in triumph and smiled broadly. Inside her thoughts exploded with joy and she wanted to burst out loud and cheer.

Brenda held on to the strong belief that her friendship with Alexander would last a lifetime. When the time came again for him to consider going back to the Soviet Union, Brenda believed in her heart that something would compel him to stay in Alaska. Hope beyond all hope was her ambitious aim. She continuously prayed for that exact situation.

The young woman did not take into account that future events might take a cruel and fateful turn away from her perceived dreams. It was inconceivable in any way that Alexander would be gone out of her life someday. How was she to know that world politics would intrude on her friendship with the handsome young Russian.

As time passed, Alexander and Brenda learned to overcome their charade in disliking each other. Underneath where it mattered the most, these two young people were actually glad to have each other for a friend. One could overcome the loneliness of a family that was lost to him forever. The other could finally relate to someone on her own age level. The necessity of companionship gradually brought them closer together.

Still they kept up the pretense of have an aversion to each other, but this was used mainly to fool the local populace and Brenda's parents. At certain times however, Alexander and Brenda would exceed their act of pretending to be just acquaintances and feelings would be hurt. Overzealous teasing at times would rear its ugly head.

The passing of time also increased Alexander's view about his own life, but was not as obvious as his feelings for Brenda. Considerable spiritual changes were taking place in his heart and mind. With the kind influences of the Hunts, Alexander's heart began opening to the possibility of a living God and to consider in the back of his mind of becoming a citizen of the United States. One thing that bothered him however was the inability to honor his mother's wishes that he return to the Soviet Union. There was also the matter of a proper burial for his parents. Alexander had no idea what had happened to the bodies of his parents after he was forced to leave and taken off Unalaska. He now wanted to ratify the matter as soon as it was possible. He languished for hours on end trying to figure a way to get out to Dutch Harbor. Authorities denied him every time because it was dangerous and isolated. There was of course the fact that the Japanese were too much of a danger to him if he were to return to Dutch Harbor.

Whenever he had a chance, Alexander would talk to Brenda about any subject, but especially about home. There was almost nothing better he wanted to do than to share his insights of the Soviet Union. Through these discussions, Alexander wrestled with differing ideologies of the United States and the Soviet Union in his mind and made some hard decisions.

Two years later, April 23, 1945

The entire Hunt family and Alexander had rented out a private room at one of Mykel's restaurants to celebrate Brenda's sixteenth birthday. A few gifts were piled on a nearby table and the family sat at another table, laughing and telling stories of Brenda in her younger days. Just then a waiter brought out a white cake with sixteen candles on it and the entire room broke out with a chorus of Happy Birthday.

Major Hunt stood up and hugged his oldest daughter from behind. "Happy birthday, sweetheart, I can't believe that you are already sixteen years old." Mr. Hunt kissed her on the cheek. "My girl is getting older. A real young woman now."

Mrs. Hunt smiled as she proceeded to hand her daughter her presents. She concurred with her husband's assessment. "Yes, she is a young woman now. Happy birthday, dear."

All her siblings replied in unison, "Happy birthday!"

Alexander just watched the proceedings and seemed to be a little nervous. In celebrating his friend's birthday, Alexander had purchased an item from the local store. He only hoped that Brenda would like his gift.

Christopher was anxious to see the treasures that his sister would receive. "Open your presents."

Carrie was just as anxious. "Yeah open them," she prodded.

"Okay," Brenda shyly responded to her brother and sister, as she reached for a medium sized present.

Just then there was a commotion outside of the celebration space. Everyone turned their attention to the door leading into the room.

Harrison abruptly burst into the room, nearly knocking over a waiter in the process. "Hey I thought I heard some singing. Well, if it isn't little Brenda Hunt, the prettiest girl in town." His words were slurred.

The major stood up to challenge the intrusion. "Harrison, this is a private party."

Harrison toppled over a rolling service tray. "Don't worry, pops, I just wanted to pay my respects to the little birthday girl."

Brenda glared at him as she crossed her arms. "Respect, that's a strange word coming from you."

Mrs. Hunt, as much as she disliked Harrison, rebuked her daughter to avoid trouble. "Brenda!"

Harrison saw that gesture as a weakness. Casually he said, "Well I might just take back that birthday greeting." He then shot an accusing glance in Alexander's direction. "I guess the commie's bad manners are rubbing off on you."

Christopher interrupted. "Look who's talking about bad manners."

Harrison remained transfixed on Alexander. "Russkie, are you still here? I would have thought that the Hunts would have wised up after two full years with you. The same goes for this town. Why do they continue to keep a dangerous foreigner around here?" His eyes shot back to the major. "…And you, Mister Hunt, should know better being that you are in the military. Didn't they teach you to spot potentially dangerous aliens?"

Major Hunt responded quickly, "I can see for myself who the dangerous one around here is, son. My job was to protect liberty, not exclude a person who wants freedom from another land."

Harrison placed his hand on his own upper hip. "Listen to me, major, you're living and playing with fire. Get smart and send the Bolshevik back to where he belongs."

The major advanced a step in Harrison's direction. "I think you better leave. Get those dangerous thoughts out of your head or you'll lose in the end."

"We'll see about that," Harrison sneered. "And you, commie," he pointed a finger at Alexander, "…if you know what's good for you, you better consider a way to get back to your homeland. We don't need any spies here."

With that verbal assault the angry young man pushed a waiter out of the way as he exited, nearly spilling the tray of food that the restaurant employee was bringing through the door.

Mr. Hunt spoke as he slowly took his seat. "His darn paranoid attitude—gets it from his dad, the two of them expect everything to revolve around them, and if they think a certain thing doesn't fit, they try every which way to get rid of it."

Mrs. Hunt spoke her mind. "Personally, I hope we don't see him for a while." She turned to look at Alexander who in her heart-felt opinion, was just like another son to her. "My dear, I am so sorry that this happened."

Alexander shrugged it off. "It's okay, Mrs. Hunt. It wasn't your fault. With all the fighting overseas, I guess I can understand why some people distrust people from other countries. With the end of the war in sight, it won't matter soon. I'll be headed home soon and Harrison won't have anything to gripe about." What he said and what he meant were two different things.

Brenda rebuffed him. "Oh no, he'll always find something to gripe about. I wish he were the one going back to the Soviet Union and not you."

Alexander decided to mock her. "You really don't want to wish that upon my country, would you?"

Brenda laughed as she adjusted her shirt. "Oh most definitely, he can leave and you can stay here."

For a moment their eyes locked upon one another. Christopher broke the spell.

"Let's forget about him. Come on, Brenda, open more of your presents."

Brenda stood for a couple of seconds and blinked her eyes. "Okay," she uttered.

Mrs. Hunt understood the implications of the delay in her voice as she eyed her daughter and the Russian.

Brenda neatly took the wrapping off the medium sized present. A beautiful green jacket was inside. "Thank you, mom and dad, it's beautiful."

Alexander reached in his pocket as he strolled over to the birthday girl. He pulled out a small neatly wrapped small box. "Brenda, I didn't want to lose your present from me among all those large presents so I put it in my pocket. Here, I hope you like it." He thrust the present at her. She carefully took it from his hand.

"Thank you." She took the wrapping off the small gift thinking in her mind that it was chewing gum or something silly. She reached in the box and pulled out a silver heart locket. Her fingers went up to her lips in surprise.

Alexander backed away slightly. "I know it's not much but I hope you like it. It's kind of small, but I don't know what girls in Alaska like for a gift."

Brenda sighed and put her hand on his arm. "It's lovely. Thank you." She proceeded to kiss him lightly on the cheek.

Alexander blushed and backed slowly away to give the siblings a chance to hand their presents to their sister.

Christopher took advantage of the awkward situation. "I never get kissed for my gift."

Brenda decided to get even for her brother's remark. "Excuse me." She reached over and kissed her brother on the cheek.

Christopher responded by using the back of his hand to wipe off the kiss like it was disgusting, but he was smiling. "Yuck, no wonder I don't get kissed. I just don't like it." His challenging eyes focused on Alexander. "I bet Alexander doesn't like it either, do you Alexander?"

Alexander opened his mouth slightly and could only blush once more. He blew out a breath of exasperated air. With insincerity in his voice, he said, "Why no... I didn't like that kissing stuff at all!"

Brenda held up the locket high in the air and looked at Alexander with soft brown eyes. "Could you help me put this on?"

Alexander glanced at everyone and knew he had no choice. He walked behind Brenda and grab both ends of the locket and hinged it together on the back of her neck as she held her hair up. Her skin was soft to the touch.

Once he was near enough to hear her whispers, Alexander heard, "Don't like kisses, Huh, you big liar. Alexander, you may never know what you like, but I think you do."

She turned sharply to face him with her eyes lowered. "Thank you for helping me to put this on."

Not wanting to give Brenda the satisfaction of knowing that she was being truthful about the words that she had whispered into his ear, Alexander made up his mind quickly to tell her it wasn't much just to annoy her, but he honestly hoped she would really love it. "It wasn't that much trouble," he scoffed. He lowered his voice so that only she could hear, "…and neither was the gift." Despite his nonchalant claim, a bead of perspiration was running down his cheek.

Brenda accepted it with a smug and feigned attitude, but secretly she put it away in a very secret place when she made it home. Her gift from Alexander was among her most precious treasures.

May 1, 1945

Affection of the two young people for each other was growing more precious every day. Upcoming events and other issues would prove to be a challenge to their long-lasting friendship.

Simplicity was hardly a way of life, but in the last year of World War II it looked as if it was part of the normal way of life for Alexander. Growing from boyhood to manhood on the surface appeared to be quite straightforward in this land of the northwest. There was sense of pride and dignity in this territory and a boy grew up to appreciate those qualities. As if fate itself had woven an unmistakable pattern, it was inevitable that Alexander was finding himself being drawn to the idea of living in the United States of America.

However, he still questioned in his mind whether it was right or wrong to try to stay in America. His father's words were constantly ringing in his ears. "The Americans are a bunch of lazy capitalists. Try to avoid them if you can. Remember they are a danger to our way of life."

Alexander, even now, struggled for a sense of identity amid a clash of cultures.

After the onset of hostilities, World War II seemed to drag on forever. The pain and suffering of the war became even more evident as gold stars replaced blue stars in the windows of many homes in Soldotna. Some loved ones would never come home.

Alexander studied the ideas of what many of these men had died for and the concept of freedom began to hold a new meaning for him.

Alexander contemplated many times what it would be like to remain in America. It actually intrigued him at times to think that it was possible.

Alexander's former countrymen in the Soviet Union didn't care where his feelings were headed. They wanted their former Ambassador's son back. Alexander, in their opinion, had been away too long from his own country. The leaders in Russia correctly assumed and were wary of the prolonged influences that Alexander might be acquiring in an alien nation. Soviet leadership wanted the boy to forget his time in Alaska and they began to pressure the United States into sending their former diplomat's son back to his homeland. The Soviet influential officials knew that the war was bound to end eventually and to leave a Soviet citizen in a potential enemy's hands was considered a major propaganda blunder.

With the renewed rumors of the war's ending increasing, pressure mounted from all sides of the political spectrum. Once the war ended, Alexander knew that he would have no excuse to disobey the Soviet leadership and their wishes and he would be sent home.

Deep inside, Alexander struggled with what he actually wanted and what he should do. The young Russian teenager needed to make a decision soon.

One powerful influence would turn the tide in Alexander's mind to try to remain in Alaska. As far as Alexander was concerned, he was safe from the ever-growing menacing influence of the Soviet government.

The Russian protests were a possible source of danger, but it was another type of threat that would permanently alter the boy's mind.

Springtime brought changes to many people in Soldotna, especially at the Hunt's residence. Brenda in the spring of 1945 was a beautiful, vivacious young lady. Her brown auburn hair was the envy of most of the girls in the town of Soldotna. Most of all it attracted many of the young men, including the overzealous bully from the States, Harrison Fisher.

Like Thomas, who sported a butch hair cut and a sloping forehead,

Harrison Fisher had developed a rough lifestyle, but he was even more aggressive with his motivation. There were rumors that Harrison had even physically hurt many people in the area where he had lived, some of it through petty extortion. His sheer size was intimidating to younger kids—many of whom had lost their lunch money to him and were afraid to admit it. Soon Harrison had his eyes set on bigger ambitions.

Once, after gaining work as a fisherman in Soldotna, one of Harrison's first objectives was to become better friends with Brenda. His stubborn arrogance would not accept defeat in any form. Aggressive as he was, it didn't take Harrison Fisher long before he lunged towards Brenda in another attempt to get her closer.

Brenda skillfully dodged his tenacious move by sitting upward just as he leaned over towards her.

"What did you do that for?" he testily snapped, not understanding her reluctance to stay clear of him.

"And why shouldn't I! You are a little too strange for my taste."

"Oh come on, baby. I'm not so bad once you get to know me."

"No, I imagine it gets even worse."

Three of the high school girls nearby squealed with laughter. Rosemary spoke out, "You won't get her to go out with you. She still has her eye on a certain foreign critter staying at her house. Not that I blame her either. That Russian is one good-looking guy."

Harrison grimaced and gave Brenda an accusing glare. "You still got that commie at your house?"

"What if I do!" she narrowed her eyes. "He's a guest and nothing more."

Rosemary continued, "But he's still a whole lot better than you... and with far better manners too!"

The girls all giggled once again.

Harrison turned and looked at them with an icy glare. He didn't like being made the fool. He stood up and walked to an empty phone booth to plot his next course of action.

Harrison's only friend, Thomas, was standing nearby. In the entire restaurant, he was the only one that had accepted the belligerent behavior of Harrison because it wasn't that much unlike his own. "Did the prettiest girl in town spurn you?" he said with a sadistic grin.

Harrison stared him down and then spoke. "Nobody will be laughing at me soon. I swear I'll make this Russian look like a creep in this town. He will pay for the indignity that I am going through. Nobody makes a fool out of me and has it easy from now on."

Thomas stated a somewhat brave comment for he feared Harrison's brute force. "So what are you going to do about it?"

"He'll live to regret this!" Harrison threatened under his breath. He hastily grabbed his fedora and turned away in anger amidst the cheers of the girls.

August 12, 1945

Mr. Hunt methodically sipped on his morning coffee as he contemplated the day's activities. "Alexander, have you seen the news?" Mrs. Hunt asked. "Look at this. The Japanese have been bombed with a weapon that has destroyed one of their major cities. The war should be over pretty soon."

Alexander had to ask, "What was the name of the city in Japan that was destroyed?"

"Hiroshima," replied Mrs. Hunt. "From what I read in the paper, the entire city was practically wiped out. The bomb must have surely shattered the fortitude of the Japanese morale," she sighed with a little reluctance. "I know the Japanese started the war, but none of the innocent people deserves what happened over there. Good Lord, there had to be women and children in that city."

"That means..." Alexander bit his bottom lip, "I can probably go home now."

Brenda looked at him with a forced smile. "I couldn't be happier for you," she weakly muttered, trying to hide her obvious disappointment.

Alexander brought his chin up in defiance. "At least the Japanese had paid for their barbaric acts. I only hope the men that killed my parents died with the others in that city. I can't imagine that they would go unpunished for what they have done to me."

Mrs. Hunt looked down to the table and back up to Alexander. "You know that there is a strong possibility that they survived the war. You can't hold what happened at Dutch Harbor against them. They were just fighting for their country."

Alexander frowned. "They don't deserve to live."

Brenda's mouth opened in disbelief. "Alexander, do you really believe what you are saying? Were your own countrymen wrong for killing? I don't like what the Japanese did any more than you did, but they were fighting for their country just like your countrymen and mine were doing. We can't blame them for hurting innocent people. The war is ending and so should the hating. We fought this war to live in peace. Are we defeating what we were fighting for? There should be an end to it now!"

Alexander lowered his head. "I only know that I cannot bring myself to forgive a race that has murdered my parents. I am glad that the Japanese were humiliated and lost the war. There is no retribution strong enough for the lifetime anguish they have given me. I really hope the men responsible for the death of my mother and father were destroyed in the fallout at either Nagasaki or Hiroshima."

Brenda was stunned. She was sure she didn't like this side of the gentle boy from Russia.

Alexander saw the hurt in Brenda's eyes. He spoke softly with his voice. "You mentioned my countrymen. A little good they did jumping into the war against Japan when it was already too late. Yeah, they did it to get more territory, but not to help save the lives of their own diplomats. Yeah, a lot of good it did for my parents."

Alexander could take the hate no longer. He broke out into tears and angrily turned away from Brenda. "I just want to be left alone."

Alexander stood in the room briefly to try and regain his composure, but he was too hurt, confused, and angry. He pushed open the screen door and marched outside.

Picking a direction to go, he walked briskly into the forest glade and up to the hill where Brenda and he had spent many quiet moments together.

Brenda started off after him and then stopped abruptly. She had momentarily thought about going after him, but realized that he needed to be alone. Hurt, she turned to the house and ran to her mother's arms. She couldn't understand the pain that Alexander was going through, but she could feel for him. She knew that she liked him more than she cared to admit.

After being comforted by her mother and looking towards the hill where Alexander was sulking, Brenda wandered to her room. Sitting on the bed, she reached over to her jewelry box.

Opening it, the young lady pulled out the gold heart locket that she had received from Alexander on her sixteenth birthday. She swung the heart, holding the chain between her thumb and forefinger. Brenda gathered it into her fist and brought it up to her lips. "If he leaves, I will never see him again." Her thoughts were painfully real. When the actual time came to say goodbye, it would be harsh for all who were involved.

The time would come soon enough.

CHAPTER 18

September 3, 1945

Victory over Japan, September 3, 1945, was a day not unexpected considering the tide of the war had turned in favor of the Allied forces, but the victory brought the paradox of both joy and anxiety to the Hunt household.

The end of World War II would soon give way and develop into the cold war, a conflict of ideas and principles between the Soviet Union and the United States. Any little factor would be cause enough for the nations to bicker at each other and Alexander immediately became a point of focus in this conflict.

Anxious for the return of their native son, Russian officials sent repeated cablegrams requesting that the boy come home, but Alexander was determined not to go back to the land of his birth. He had learned to appreciate his newfound freedom and he suspected that life would not be so pleasant for him if he returned to the Soviet Union. The inevitable confrontation was beginning to emerge.

There was also one important consideration for his decision that he couldn't ignore. Alexander was falling in love with Brenda.

Major Hunt strolled into the living room that morning where Brenda, Alexander, and Mrs. Hunt were sitting and talking about the day's expectations and announced, "Alexander, the State Department called today. It seems like you are on your way home, my boy. The official surrender of the Japanese was signed yesterday at Tokyo Bay aboard the battleship *Missouri*. We don't have to worry about the Japanese preventing you from heading to your country any longer and there is no reason to keep you from going home now." His finger went up to wipe a single tear away from his eye. "We're going to miss you."

The family sat in silence waiting for a reaction from Alexander who sat dumbfounded. Brenda glanced up with her brown eyes full of tears. "I didn't think it would happen this soon. I mean I am glad that the Japanese have been defeated, but I was hoping that you could have stayed around a little bit longer."

Alexander smiled at Brenda. "An overbearing, obnoxious, scalawag like me, why would you want that to happen?"

"You kind of grow on a person. You are not that bad of a chap, even for being a Russian."

Alexander looked down into her brown eyes that reminded him of the eyes of a gentle fawn. Like always, they were beautiful. Having lived in both worlds, Alexander was still wondering if he did want to go back to the Soviet Union. He thought once more of his mother's wishes. The emotional strain of this heart-wrenching decision was nearly tearing at his insides.

Alexander had made some comparisons between Russia and the United States and he was starting to have his doubts. As much as he loved his former country, Alexander knew that Stalin was a cruel and hateful dictator, almost as bad as Hitler. It was hard for him to finally admit it in his heart, but he understood that there was political corruption in the Soviet Union that they didn't have in the United States.

"I have to admit, though, that I trusted my father immensely and that includes what he said about America. He couldn't have been wrong. He couldn't have?"

Brenda heard him as he repeated the words. She responded, "But you are so sure that your father was right in what he said about Americans?"

"He was like all the other Russians. He believed what he had been told. I can see now that, even though I loved my father very much, I cannot agree with his political philosophy. I have seen and heard too much here in this American territory that contradicts almost everything that he had taught me about capitalism. The communist party buried many lies deep in our mind."

Alexander thrust his eyes upwards. "I can see now that my father would have believed the truth about America if only he lived long enough to experience the freedom and people that exist here. I want to stay here. I want to know that I have made the right choice. I want to live, serve, and love in this adopted land of my choosing. I want what you call political asylum."

Major Hunt interjected some of his own thoughts. "Alexander, it is not as easy as what you are making it out to stay in the United States. There are major complications."

"Such as?"

"Such as getting the approval of our own government, and I'm positive that your own countrymen will have quite a few objections."

"But if there is any chance at all, I want to try."

Mr. Hunt nodded. "Well, all we can do is try. I'll make some calls and we'll see what can be done."

Mrs. Hunt hugged Alexander. "Yes, we can try. We'll see what our people at the State Department will have to say."

Alexander had to ask one more question. "Has this ever been done before?"

Mr. Hunt halfway smiled. "It's a little late to be asking that now, but yes, it has been done before."

It wasn't long after the conversation that the process for Alexander's request for asylum were put into motion. Arrangements were made to meet with U.S. officials the next day. The men of the State Department were dumbfounded and appalled for they knew that the Russians would never believe that one of their own would want to stay in the United States voluntarily. Diplomatically, the pressure from the Soviet government was immense. Repeated requests poured into the State Department. The Russians were already beginning to press the matter and kept asking about the boy's welfare.

The State Department sent men to convince him to leave. Alexander had put them into a perilous position with the Soviets who were now demanding that their wayward lamb be sent home.

The U.S. State Department men sounded desperate as they stated their objections to Alexander of his consideration to stay. "You must go home. The war is over. Your own country wants you back now," the top official implored as he wiped perspiration from his forehead.

Alexander sighed, but his resolve was still with him. He had to convince these men that he was not leaving on his own accord.

CHAPTER 19

Alexander's eyes went downcast in displeasure. He had no wish to leave his adopted land and he had grown quite fond of both Brenda and the Hunts. He was determined to stay.

Suddenly a flash of a motivational notion came to him. *This is my life and I can do anything that I want with it,* his thoughts were bold. *I'm going to tell them, NO!*

Alexander sat defiantly in his chair. "I refuse to leave, but if you want the Soviets to know that I am sincere about staying here, then invite some of the Russian government officials here to Alaska so that they can see for themselves that I want to stay. They will see what are my true intentions really are in this matter."

"But you must return to your homeland," the men insisted. "You are making it very difficult for everyone involved. You cannot stay here."

Alexander shook his head. "Why?" Alexander looked bewildered. "Haven't you given freedom to others from my old country before?"

"You must understand, Alexander, we are on very shaky ground with the Soviets as it is. If we allow you to stay, diplomatic conditions will be sure to disintegrate between your country and ours. Now that the war is over, we must in all good consciousness do our utmost to keep the peace. You have no choice in the matter."

"No. I am not going back."

The government men looked at each other, each showing a slight smile. They had been through this before with other people seeking freedom. The State men shrugged their shoulders and agreed to the terms. "However," they said, "if the Soviet delegation gives us just cause that you should not remain here, we will have to consider other options."

"Fair enough," Alexander nodded.

"Oh, we must tell you that a delegation from the Soviet Union is coming here in one week to check up on you. They want to see if you are okay and not…" The government official cleared his throat. "(Ahem) mentally unbalanced. They want to talk to you and they want most of all to take you back to their country. We are under an obligation to let them see you."

Alexander nodded with a nervous frown. "I see, but you will be with me while they are here."

"Of course we will."

The American officials could see now that Alexander was serious and meant what he said. Now if they could only convince the Soviet delegation. Japan had lost the conflict and the American delegation could no longer use the war as an excuse to keep Alexander in their country. They had to let the Soviet officials see for themselves that Alexander was willing to become an American citizen.

Alexander shook his head and winked at his adopted family. The Hunts just smiled back. Permission for the young Russian to stay in the United States was granted.

Trying to stall for time, the American government would claim that major health problems were keeping Alexander from coming back to the Soviet Union for the time being.

March 17, 1946

Reaction from the authorities in the Soviet Union of the defection was swift. Angry words floated back and forth between the two super powers over the boy's future. Alexander's situation was becoming critical in the eyes of his old countrymen. To let him go would encourage others from their homeland to leave. Alexander's status was now becoming an international incident and the Russians accused the Americans of deliberately holding a Soviet citizen against his will. Nor were they satisfied when they were allowed to see him and ask him personally if he wanted to stay. The Russian delegation believed that the boy had been drugged and his mind had been altered somehow. The American government desperately tried to convince the young man to return to his own country.

The Soviets were just as determined as the statesmen were to bring back the son of their former Alaskan diplomat. They stated plainly to the young man, "No more of this foolishness. You are going back to the Soviet Union with us!"

"No!" said Alexander in defiance. "I have my reasons for staying in this land. One of the major reasons is the disregard that the Soviet leaders have for their own people. If the Soviet Union is so great, why are people forced to live there against their will? In this country, people are free to go anywhere, come or do whatever they want."

"Are they allowed to steal or kill at any time?" snapped one of the Russian officials.

"You know what I mean!" Alexander replied frowning at his Russian countrymen. "My father and mother died in this country, not by the hands of the Nazis, but by the hands of the Japanese. Russia is brave enough to defend her own soil, but when it comes to helping our allies in the Pacific, the Russians denied aid even though the Americans provided lend-lease supplies. Is that what it means to be a communist? Doing things for our own satisfaction?"

"Was America willing to fight on our side when Herr Hitler first attacked Russia?" one of the men reminded Alexander. "Who fought alone for so long?"

The Russian men bitterly resented the manner in which Alexander thrust the question at them. "Well, it certainly wasn't the Americans."

Alexander narrowed the slits of his eyes. "It seems to me that the British were fighting alone while Stalin was making friends with the German dictator, just so they could divide Poland between the two of them. Does that sound like a nation that is concerned about all the people of this world or their own self worth? No, gentlemen, if I am to make a wise decision and know which country is better for my situation, I must live here to determine for myself which is right for me."

The head man of the Russian delegation, Ivan Niecholeiyev-ich, moved closer to the young man. Almost nose-to-nose with the young Russian, Niecholeiyevich looked squarely in the eyes of Alexander and spoke to him in whispered Russian. "If you decide to stay here, my young friend, maybe one day you will live to regret it. Think about that, Alexander. Think about it very hard. Make a wise decision. We will be keeping in close contact with you."

Niecohleiyevich whipped his head towards the Americans who were standing nearby just within earshot. It was obvious that he suspected them of influencing his young countryman. "You must convince him to come back to the Soviet Union with us. We are warning you now that if your government wishes for non-compliance of these matters, there will be grave and dire consequences between our two countries and our two peoples."

He turned once again to Alexander in an intimidating manner. "Remember well, my young friend, what I am saying to you now." Niecholeiyevich grinned nastily. "I am sure that you only wish what is best for Alexander... and his safety." The grin faded into a grisly frown. "Consider seriously what I am telling you. I will see you soon."

Infuriated, Niecholeiyevich and the Soviet delegation left after one more strict command that the boy be returned to Russia at the earliest convenience.

The Americans who were listening to the Russian tirade watched his departure with chagrin. Hearing what they perceived were explicit threats, the statesmen for the United States were convinced that Alexander needed asylum in Alaska.

"We can see now that it would not be wise or prudent to send you back to your homeland. We will work right away on protected status for you. We will need some information if you wish to get started."

Not only did the nasty attitude of the Russian delegation help Alexander's cause, but other events helped the situation. The young Russian would be allowed to stay because the Americans and the

Russians had more pressing matters they had to deal with, primarily the partitioning of Berlin and Germany. This small lull would not last long.

May 23, 1946

Alexander was bitter, not so much that the U.S. government was so protective of him, but they still had deprived him of his right to bury his parents properly. His feeling of helplessness was further enhanced by the idea that he could have done more under his own initiative. He felt that he owed no one anything. This feeling even carried partly over to the Hunts. They had been very kind to him, but they were also supporting the government's decision to keep him from going back to the Soviet Union.

Alexander, in his confusion, tried to act tough in front of his benefactors in Soldotna. "I don't know what it means to be kind," he told Brenda. "People have always taken the things I loved away from me."

"That's not true," Brenda protested. "Who gave you a place to stay when your parents were killed? Who gave you asylum when you wanted it?"

"But those things were not the things I loved. You need to understand. I loved my home in the Soviet Union, but the government prevents me from living there the way I really want to live. If it weren't for them, I would be living in Leningrad, the city of my father."

"Alexander, you will have to make up your own mind how and when you want to go on. You are the only one that can determine where you go and that decision will affect the rest of your life. Be wise and prudent in what course you will take."

Alexander watched as Brenda trudged back to her house. Alexander lifted his eyes skyward and watched the clouds moving swiftly across the golden sky. "If you exist, why confront me now? Is my life a ball of clay, a play toy only to be shaped when you want it molded for your pleasure? Where do I go from here?"

Alexander looked to the one place to find his answers. The deep forest beckoned to him and he retreated towards them. He started down a deserted road near the main highway.

In his solitude, which flooded his brain with various memories of the past, Alexander failed to notice a dark black van slowly driving nearby.

Two sinister looking men peered out of the window to see if others were nearby. They continued to roll closer to their unsuspecting quarry. The vehicle rolled slowly as if guided by a delicate strand of thread. Alexander looked up briefly and noticed that the van was pulling over to a nearby curb. What was strange was that the drivers had not bothered to turn off the motor even after the van had apparently been parked. Alexander put his hands in his pockets and began to walk back towards the house. The soft crunch of the gravel beneath his feet was interrupted by the distant noise of a slow moving vehicle. The black vehicle continued to follow the Russian boy for quite a while and soon Alexander finally realized that he was being stalked. He began to quicken his pace, but the large panel vehicle raced ahead and blocked his path.

Alexander sensed that something was terribly wrong, but before he could react, two men jumped out of the van and grabbed him.

Alexander struggled, but the men were too powerful. Alexander's struggle to free himself almost succeeded, but the Soviets were men who had trained daily in physical conditioning. They were too strong. They started dragging the young man to the van.

"Craig! Christopher! Help!" Alexander finally grasped the seriousness of his plight.

The more powerful of the men clamped his hand over Alexander's mouth and whispered, "You were warned."

Alexander reacted quickly. Using his elbow, Alexander jammed a backwards slash into the jaw of the first man. With another quick thrust of his free hand, he was able to break free of one man's grip and hit him. It was to no avail. This only encouraged the second man to hold on tighter. Alexander elbowed him in the stomach and tripped as he tried to run. Before he could completely get away, the other agent grabbed him from behind and held firm. Alexander was trapped. Both men were now holding him in a stranglehold. Alexander could barely move. The Russians gripped him tighter as they pulled him closer to the van. Alexander could see ropes inside the paneled vehicle. Alexander knew that if these men were able to force him into the van, he would never see Alaska again.

CHAPTER 20

Alexander attempted to hit the larger man with his elbow, but the Soviet agent was much too fast for the young Russian teenager. The muscular kidnapper eluded Alexander's blow and reacted with one of his own. With a lightning reflex type of punch, he clobbered Alexander in the stomach. Alexander stumbled briefly and looked up just in time to see a fist slam him in the face. The other man had recovered from his blow and was now helping the second assailant grab Alexander. Even though he was stunned, Alexander tried to hit the two men who were dragging him towards the van with its side panel door open. By their manners and appearance, Alexander suspected right away that these two buffoons were KGB agents trying to take him back to the Soviet Union.

Alexander felt another blow to the back of his head. Slightly dazed by the final hit to the back of his head, he couldn't resist the men as they began to drag him closer towards the van.

Suddenly one of the men loosened his grip on the young Russian. He turned in response to someone that Alexander could not see. Alexander could hear the steady sound of running feet of two men approaching from behind him. Alexander then heard a shout.

"Hey, what are two think you are trying to do?" came a yell from one of the men coming in headlong into the melee of the gathering on the street.

Alexander shook off the grogginess he had been feeling. He could tell that the yelling was from his two friends from the fishing fleet, Craig and Paul.

Alexander resisted by bracing his feet against the pavement. Even in struggling with the man in the trench coat, Alexander was able to see from the corner of his eye that it was indeed his two best friends and co-workers.

Craig and Paul ran up, dropped, and rolled into the would-be kidnappers. Knocking them down, Alexander broke free from the grip of the Soviets and turned to face his attackers.

The Russians buckled to the ground and came up on their knees in a slight daze. The first thing they noticed was that both of the young Alaskan men were larger than them. The Russians gauged their chances and they decided to fight it out using other means.

The Soviets quickly got back on their feet. As they began to reach into their overcoats, apparently to pull out some weapons, the sound of a police siren pierced the air.

The two men looked at each other and decided that the risk of finishing off their former countryman was not worth the risk of being caught by the local authorities. Miffed by the humiliation, they ran to the van. Craig, Paul and Alexander ran after the kidnappers. The Russians were fast enough to get into their vehicle before their pursuers arrived. Before Craig and Paul could run down the wooden paneled truck, the vehicle squealed its wheels and fired off down the road. It disappeared quickly down a side street that led out of the town.

Alexander brushed dust from the road off himself. "Hey guys, I appreciate what you just did for me."

"Don't mention it, Alexander." Paul shook his head in a teasing manner and smiled. "I just don't know about you, I mean, we just can't leave you alone for a minute without you getting into trouble."

Craig laughed. "I guess you're a hopeless case." He shifted his eyes down the street. "Who were those guys anyway?"

"I'm pretty sure they were Russian agents sent here to take me back to the Soviet Union. They must want me pretty bad. What a shame they can't catch me." Alexander laughed nervously, and then his face went serious once again. He knew how close he was to being sent back to the Soviet Union. "Let's just hope they don't try this again." Alexander looked bewildered. "What are you guys doing here anyway? How is it that you two suddenly decide to show up?"

"Major Hunt sent us down here. He saw the van follow you after you left his house. He suspected that they were up to no good, so he sent us after you."

"Well, it looks like you arrived just in the nick of time and I am grateful."

"No problem." Paul rolled his eyes in an attempt to make light of the harrowing experience.

Alexander looked down to his feet, feeling quite embarrassed about being taken so easily, especially after he had been told to be careful. "I guess I should watch my step from now on."

"That would be a good idea," Craig answered. "If they tried it once, they might try it again."

May 29, 1946

The night was cool, but Brenda went out without a sweater. She peered up at the night sky. The breeze from the ocean swept across her back yard in soft patterns. Still with such a peaceful night, there was concern lurking inside of her. There had been no word from the authorities of how they would handle the near kidnapping of Alexander. What was even worse was the fact that there was no mention of the fate of the two Soviet kidnappers. "Were they caught? Would they come back again to maybe even try and kill Alexander?" The questions bothered her. It worried her that the handsome young man staying with her family was in so much trouble. Her feelings for him were growing stronger, although she didn't want to admit it to anyone, even her closest friends.

Looking up at the glittering patterns of bright pin points of lights up above her, Brenda was caught momentarily in a daze. The stillness of the night was only interrupted by the soft chirping of crickets in the nearby field.

The young woman's memories of the last four years were sweet ones. Brenda was happy that the Russian boy was still around. So deep in thought, she was unaware that a pair of eyes were watching her every move in the back yard. The sound of the crickets suddenly went silent.

As she stepped out further into the yard, Brenda heard the crack of a dry limb. She looked up to see a strange man climbing over the fence. She rapidly brought the back of her hand to her mouth as she started to flee. In sheer panic, she turned to the house. In a loud voice, she cried out, "Dad, Mom, call the police." She ran in and locked the door. Frightened, Brenda peered out a side window and saw the man lunging towards the closed door.

CHAPTER 21

Mr. and Mrs. Hunt were beginning to rise from their seats in the living room when a loud knock resounded from the front door. The major grabbed a nearby walking stick. "Yes, who is it?"

"Federal authorities," came back the reply.

Mr. Hunt cautiously approached the door. "How do I know that?"

"We were sent by Ike Gorman."

Mr. Hunt nodded to the rest of the family. "It's okay."

"But Dad, there is someone in the back yard."

"He must be a Federal agent as well," the major stated with a hint of hesitation, hoping somehow his words were true. He slowly opened the door.

The Federal agents were invited to come in. Their guns were drawn as they entered the house. "Is Alexander here?" they demanded.

"Yes," replied Mrs. Hunt with concern in her voice. "Did he do something wrong?"

"No, ma'am. We are just taking precautionary measures. He needs to come with us."

"Would it be too much to ask for your IDs!" she said firmly, but gently.

"No, ma'am." The men pulled out their badges and IDs.

Mrs. Hunt sighed with relief. She now understood that the men had their weapons drawn to protect young Alexander.

"Why are you here?" she asked again, hoping that it wasn't to take the young man away. She knew that this could either mean trouble or something was about to change. With everything that had happened, it was apparent that the Russian government was trying to get Alexander back into their country. It was more than apparent that he needed to be hidden away for a while.

"We are here to take Alexander with us. Mrs. Hunt, you need to understand that unless Alexander finds safety elsewhere, the Soviets will be back to try to kidnap him again. We are here to insure that doesn't happen again."

"But where are you taking him?" asked Christopher, the older brother, with concern in his voice.

"We will conceal him somewhere he will be safe. We can't tell you where, and to tell the truth he needs to go now."

"You want me to leave now, right at this moment?" The young Russian had just come out of a back room and looked around at everyone in disbelief. His eyes went downcast and there suddenly was a great sadness felt throughout the room. He was stunned at first, but moved quickly to pack his clothes. Alexander was given little warning that he would be going and it unnerved him. The young Russian could understand why he had to leave, but it did not make it any easier to know that. The price was high and he was beginning to feel like he was actually part of the Hunt family and now he was being separated from them. There was little time to say, "Goodbye."

"I want to thank you for giving me refuge after the death of my parents. I appreciate all that you have done. I will never forget it."

Mrs. Hunt slowly lifted her head out of a closed hand to her mouth. "Will there be a possibility that we will see you again?"

The men shrugged in a non-compliance gesture.

Alexander glanced over to the men who would be whisking him away. "I don't know. It would be nice to say that I will be coming back, but I don't know where I will end up." Alexander looked at his adopted family, especially at Brenda. "I will miss you all terribly."

Brenda couldn't control the gnawing pain creeping into her stomach. Tears started seeping into her tear ducts. She flung her hand to her face. She couldn't let Alexander know that she was going to miss him. After all he was a rude Russian boy, a rude, but mighty handsome Russian boy.

Alexander hugged the major and his wife. He then came up to Brenda. "Goodbye, Brenda. I bet you'll be glad to get me out of your hair for a while."

"You know it," she replied trying to hide her disappointment.

Alexander noticed her moist eyes. "Oh, you'll miss me and you know it," he spouted arrogantly.

Brenda grumbled back, "Miss you? I rather miss a toad." She softened her stance. "Take care of yourself, will ya?"

"I promise," he smiled softly.

Brenda hesitated, but just for a moment. With her arms stretched out, she responded by giving him an extended and warm embrace. The softness of her body was pleasant to Alexander. His feelings had changed dramatically for her in the last four years.

Alexander released his embrace. "I guess I'm ready to go," he said to everyone. He picked up his bags. "I will miss you all." His eyes shifted from the parents back to Brenda. "Please don't forget me."

He was out the door before anyone could say, "We won't!"

Brenda sniffed and looked with a solemn gaze towards her father. "Will we ever see him again?"

"I don't think so, sweetheart," he replied softly.

It had all happened so fast. Brenda was at a loss. A huge lump in her throat blocked her protests. Unable to speak, Brenda went to her room and closed the door behind her.

The major and his wife looked at each other with disappointment in their eyes. Mrs. Hunt spoke first, "I know this is breaking her heart."

The major responded, "I know, but he will be in a safer place now. She'll get over it."

Mrs. Hunt slowly shook her head, "I'm not too sure about that."

Upstairs, Brenda was showing her displeasure. As she nearly slammed her door, vibrations rattled some of her personal items. Hanging near her mirror was the golden locket that Alexander had given her. It swung back and forth like a pendulum. The young girl slowly reached up for the piece of jewelry and closed her hand around it. Clutching the locket, Brenda brought it up to her chest and closed her eyes in remembrance.

Fighting hard for composure, she finally gave in to her true feelings. The tears poured out.

CHAPTER 22

Four days later.
A plot of acreage outside of Bozeman, Montana.

"Welcome to your new home," the agent pointed as he let Alexander out of the car, his finger aimed at a small log house with a veranda on two sides.

Alexander looked around at the tall ponderosa pines. "Well, it seems nice, but where am I?"

"Are you going to promise you won't try to contact anyone and let them know where you are hiding?"

"Yes, I promise. I remember I'm not even supposed to contact the Hunts."

"Good. We're in southwest Montana near a town called Bozeman. You will start working tomorrow at the park south of here called Yellowstone. You will go under the name of Alex Evans, a young college student from Denver, Colorado. It has all been arranged. Identification papers, job permit, park pass, background cover. It is up to you to adjust and adjust quickly. Your main job is to maintain a low profile and don't get too chummy with the local population."

"What if I get bored?"

"We'll keep you busy. Hopefully the Russians will quit looking for you after a while. They have no idea where you are and I want it to stay that way. Do you understand?"

"Yeah." Alexander regarded the man like an overzealous school principal.

"Some of your things are still outside."

Alexander held up his hand, "I'll go get them. You just stay here and make your calls."

Alexander ambled out to the darkened vehicle. It was somewhat isolated where the handsome young Russian was, but he could see some houses in the distance. He could also see that a young lady was walking up the road towards him.

Alexander quickly averted his eyes to avoid a conversation. *What a stupid thing to do,* he quickly figured out in his mind. Alexander wanted to ignore her but thought it would arouse her suspicions if he just pretended that she wasn't there. He turned to face her. "Hi," he uttered.

She was tall and slender with long blonde wavy hair that was curled at the ends. She had some front teeth that stuck out slightly but she was still quite pretty. She continued to advance towards him. "Hi, are you new to the area?"

"Yeah, I just moved in today."

She smiled in response, "Welcome to Bozeman. Are you working in town?"

"No, I'm working for the National Park Service at Yellowstone."

"That's great. I handle the west entrance gate admissions. Maybe I'll be seeing you there."

"It's possible," he smiled. This girl was quite lovely and charming. "My name is Alexan.... Alex Evans."

She noticed the slight mistake, but ignored it. "My name's Jeannette – Jeannette Swayne. It's nice to meet you."

"Same here. Do you live nearby?"

"Right up at that white house. That's where I live. Where are you from?"

"Denver. Denver, Colorado."

"Not too far from home, just a couple of states away." She waited for a response, but received none. "Well, I know you are new here and I'm just a stranger to you, but would you mind if I come and visit from time to time?" She noticed his hesitation. "Is that okay?"

He didn't want to raise her suspicions. "Oh, sure—anytime."

She brought her forefinger up to the corner of her mouth. "Oh, by the way, you said you are from Denver?"

"Yes, that's correct."

"Have you ever been to Sam Houston's grave on Lookout Mountain?"

"Uhh, yeah, a few times."

She frowned at his ignorance. "Oh really. I believe that is Buffalo Bill up there, not Sam Houston. Are you sure you are from Denver?"

Alexander swallowed hard and turned quickly. He narrowed his eyes for he knew that she had tricked him. He turned to his new home. "You know what; I have a lot of errands to run. I need to get going."

Jeannette eyed him suspiciously and backed up slowly. "Okay, see ya later."

Alexander nodded with a crooked mouth. "Yeah, sure." Looking back, but quickening his pace, Alexander thought, "That girl is going to be a lot of trouble to me."

Soldotna, Alaska

Brenda was curled up on the family sofa reading a magazine. A soft light from a nearby lamp flooded the quiet room. She lay down the book in deep thought. "I wonder how Alexander is doing," she asked her mother who was ironing.

"I don't know, but I think I saw some goons looking for him today. I made a call to the police. I'm glad he's not around."

"They won't find him. They won't find him ever."

Mrs. Hunt lifted her eyes to meet those of her daughter's. "He should be fine. If they let us hear from him, it will be okay, but it's better this way."

"How can you say that, Mother? He had a good life here."

"Yeah, it's too bad that no one around here likes him that much."

"What do the town people know? Some of them never knew him that well."

"I'm not talking about the townspeople. I'm talking about you. You were always picking on the poor boy."

"I wouldn't do that now. Not in a million years."

"You mean you might like him."

Brenda looked at her mother with a half grin. "Maybe!"

Mrs. Hunt smiled. "I'm sure he would be glad to hear you say that. But for the time being, I'm glad he's far from here."

"I guess I am too. At least he is safe now, wherever he is living now."

Mrs. Hunt leaned on the table with her elbows and fingers grasped in a tight embrace. "I know for a fact that his destination lies in the hands of another."

Brenda smiled slightly. "I know that, Mother, but it doesn't make it any easier for me."

Brenda drifted to her room and wondered where Alexander was and if he was happy being away from the Hunts. "Don't stay away too long!" she whispered into the air. "I miss you." She opened her window and gazed up into the stars wondering which one was right above him. She wished that she could ride on top of it just to see where he was and to make sure that he was okay. She closed her eyes trying to envision Alexander's face. She wanted to see his brown eyes and bright smile one more time.

Bozeman, Montana. The same night.

One of the American agents protecting the young Russian came by the cabin and had some good news for Alexander, although it was only a partial blessing. "We have captured a red agent near Soldotna, but he refuses to tell us where his partner is hiding. You may be here for a long time."

Alexander sighed in disappointment. "Thanks. Keep me informed."

The agent nodded and by hand signal let the Russian know that he was going to drive away.

After the agent left, Alexander leaned against the pine pole that was part of the foundation of his porch. He focused his gaze towards the heavens as a shooting star danced across the night sky.

As Alexander scanned the night sky, he wondered if perhaps his destination could be in the hands of someone else. He had never thought that loneliness would be such a problem so early in his life again. His eyes turned to the northwest sky. Alaska was in that direction somewhere. He longed to be near the Hunts once again. His heart swelled with sadness, but a glint of hope remained. The image of Brenda crossed his mind again and again. "Some day it will happen. If nothing else occurs in my lifetime, I make this solemn promise to myself. Some day, I will see you again."

A distant howl of a coyote made him sit up and take notice. The young man frowned and thought, "Even the coyote is miserable by himself."

Alexander slowly closed his eyes and placed his head against the front post and tried to stifle the pain in his heart. He had lost another family and he was quite alone once more.

Seething determination once more entered his heart. Fresh air of the nearby pine trees entered his lungs as he took in a deep breath contemplating the past and the future. This instinctive motion had been a recurring factor in coping with so many losses.

The young man peered at the beauty of the quarter moon and scanned the northern starry sky. In his deepest dreams and self-proclaimed desires, Alexander knew one day he would return to the land called Alaska.